# STONEY LONESOME ROAD

*a Novel*

*Rick Pendergast*

ISBN: 0692990747
ISBN 13: 9780692990742
Library of Congress Control Number: 2017918529
Rick Pendergast, Eau Claire, WI

# DEDICATIONS

*I dedicate this book to the memory of my Mother and Dad, James and Beverly Pendergast. To paraphrase Abraham Lincoln, all I am or all I ever hope to be, I owe to those good people.*

## Nothing Gold Can Stay
### By Robert Frost

Nature's first green is gold,
Her hardest hue to hold.
Her early leaf's a flower;
But only so an hour.
So leaf subsides to leaf.
So Eden sank to grief,
So dawn goes down to day.
Nothing gold can stay.

# CHAPTER ONE

Jack Delaney hated wearing a tie. All the same, he tied a perfect knot. Tonight's retirement dinner in his honor was to be a celebration of thirty-five years on the Brunswick Sheriff's Department. He was dismayed that his career was over. It seemed like yesterday that he was sworn in as a rookie. Jack reached down and ruffled the fur on his big dog's head. Harry licked his hand. He wore his best pair of cowboy boots for the occasion. With them on, Jack Delaney rounded up to an even six foot.

At the door, he pulled on his coat and gave Harry a scratch. "See you in a bit, old dog." Then he was out the door and down his neatly shoveled sidewalk to the garage. It was a short drive downtown to the Masonic Temple. Policemen mingled with courthouse personnel to wish him farewell. Although he appreciated the effort, Jack would rather have just left quietly with no party.

During the cocktail hour he mingled with people he'd worked with for all these years. They shook his hand and said nice things. Retired and active cops congratulated, teased, and praised him. Friends and neighbors wished him the best. Father Dan, the official chaplain of the Sheriff's Department, was sober. He had been asked to give the prayer before the dinner so he stayed away from the sauce, for now. He heartily shook Jack's hand and moving in close whispered in his ear that he had a joke to tell him later. Father Dan was known for his big heart, boozing, faux Irish brogue, and an occasional raunchy joke. Jack told him he looked forward to hearing it.

During the dinner and short program more praise was heaped on the retired detective. The sheriff presented him with a Certificate of Recognition that stated, among other things, that Jack had solved every major case assigned to him as a detective. The crowd was also reminded that Jack had been Police Officer of the Year twice during his career.

Cries of "Speech, speech, speech" prompted Jack to say a few words of gratitude. As he did so, he noticed Cindy Robertson smiling at him from the center table. She was seated with Mattie Graves, the widow Fitzgerald, and some other friends. He didn't see Will Graves, but wasn't surprised that he didn't attend. His dementia would have left him confused and lost.

As duty demanded, Jack stayed until the end of the party. When it was finally over he thankfully headed for his old blue truck and home. When he got to the truck Cindy Robertson was waiting for him. "Stopping by tonight Jack," she asked. He could tell that she'd had a few drinks. When that happened her warm nature grew warmer. It was not unusual for him to stop and see Cindy on occasion. Sometimes it was more frequent than others.

"Well, I suppose so. It is the holiday season and all...," he answered, but was interrupted with a kiss. "See you at my place," Cindy said as she went off to her car. Jack waved goodnight to a couple of staggering cops and climbed into old blue for the drive to Cindy's place.

She lived above the bar where Jack grew up. Cindy had taken over the bar when his dad became sick. By the time he got there she had the place lit softly with tiny white Christmas lights. Candles were burning and the wine was open.

"Looks like you're expecting company," he said, accepting a glass of wine and another kiss.

"And I suppose you think that someone is you?"

It was snowing soft and steady when Jack left Cindy's the next morning. Harry was happy to see him. First Jack made a pot of coffee, then changed his clothes. When Jack let Harry back into the house, the big dog was covered with snow. He lit a fire in his small fireplace and settled into his chair with coffee in hand. He looked through the retirement cards and made a mental note to pick up some "thank you" cards.

Then he picked up the Certificate of Recognition given to him at his retirement party and read through the text. He stopped and reread the line that praised him for solving every one of the major cases assigned to him. He took his pen and circled the section that said "every one" and wrote next to it "all but one."

For thirty-five years Jack Delaney had attempted to solve the murder of Sonny Howland. He was shot and killed in 1950 out at Dismal Creek. The murder was never solved. Jack spent his entire career looking for the answer. A small caliber hand gun had been used, but never found. There were no witnesses and no one ever came forward.

But it was not the identity of the victim that intrigued and inspired Jack to spend so much time on one case. Sonny Howland, a charmer and a tough guy, fought and drank his way around the county. He was disliked by nearly as many people who liked him. Rather, it was the universal belief that Will Graves was the killer that inspired his professional odyssey. Although it was never proven that Will was the killer, the consensus in the community was that Will had done the deed. Most people concluded that Will had killed Howland as a result of the long standing feud between the Howland and Graves families that finally erupted into a fist fight one night at Hank's Place.

Although the murder occurred when Jack was a toddler, he heard about it occasionally over the years. Long before he became a policeman, Jack was interested in the case. His close association with Will and Mattie Graves intensified his curiosity.

His heart told him that Will Graves did not kill Sonny Howland. It went against everything he knew about him. It was not that Will was incapable of killing someone. Rather, if he had done so, he would have owned up to it. He was a man who faced responsibility square in the face. Jack Delaney believed that Will Graves was the most honest and fair minded man he had ever known. It went against his character to have committed the crime and then to have avoided the time. So for thirty-five years he tried and failed to clear Will's name. Although Jack was satisfied with his career in general, he was deeply disappointed that he had failed to solve the case. He felt that he had let Will Graves down.

His interest in clearing Will's name and solving the murder had been the initial reason that he had gone into law enforcement in the first place. Now his career was over and it appeared that the case, now fifty years old and counting, would never be cleared. It also appeared that the taint of the murder would follow Will Graves into the ground, and would haunt Jack Delaney for the rest of his days.

# CHAPTER TWO

The retirement party, while nice, proved anticlimactic. For Jack, the real end of his career came when he turned in his badge. This last official act had left him feeling naked and diminished. He had worn his police identity with pride and humility for thirty-five years. The responsibility for lives and liberty had been his purpose. Without that purpose, Jack felt lost. His good friend Will Graves always said "You've got to have a reason to get up in the morning." Jack wondered what his reason would be to get up in the morning now. He already missed the weight of the badge in his coat pocket.

He would never forget the first time he put on the badge and felt the weight it carried. When the sheriff handed it to him he said "there are two ways you can wear this badge, son. You can use it to push people around or use it to protect and serve. Only you can decide which it will be." His first day on the job, Jack saved a life. On his last day on the job he changed a light bulb for Mattie Graves. He thought that those two days were appropriate bookends to his "protect and serve" law enforcement career.

On the first day of his law enforcement career, he saved Doyle Howland's life. Doyle was the son of the murdered Sonny Howland. After getting his badge, he was sent out on the road. He was told to "stay out of trouble" and write a few traffic warnings.

Armed with the barest knowledge from a six week recruit school, he set out on his thirty-five year career. His maiden voyage took him to familiar territory. First he stopped at Hank's Place on the corner of the highway and Stoney Lonesome Road. Hank was his father and the sole proprietor of the long running local country tavern. They lived in the small apartment above the bar.

Hank was behind the bar when Jack walked in wearing his new uniform. Everyone in the bar knew him because he grew up in the place. He had tended bar along side his dad for many years. Uncharacteristically, Hank came out from behind the bar and shook his hand. In front of everyone Hank announced, "Son, I'm proud of you." Jack had been so surprised he could think of nothing to say. It was the first time in his entire life that his father had praised him for anything.

Shocked, pleased, and more than a little embarrassed Jack left the bar after enduring equal amounts of congratulations and good-natured grief. He could not believe that his father had not only praised him, but had done so in front of the hometown crowd. His father had raised him basically alone, and warm fuzzies were not part of the equation. Criticism delivered with sharpness was the common teaching method of his father. And this one instance of praise turned out to be the only one he ever got from the old man.

Although Jack respected and loved his dad, to say that they were close would have been an enormous stretch. When he was appointed deputy, Jack made a promise to himself he never broke. He would never again, for the rest of his life, tend bar. Not for his dad. Not for anybody.

Feeling self conscious in his uniform and squad car, Jack opted to get as far away from people as he could. Upon leaving the parking lot, Jack turned west on Stoney Lonesome Road. As he drove along the familiar country road he began to relax and enjoy his new status. Upon seeing smoke coming from over the rise, Jack called it in and went to investigate. When he got close enough he saw that Doyle Howland's trailer was on fire. Doyle had been a regular at Hank's Place so Jack had known him all his life. He was pretty sure Doyle had to be inside the trailer because his rusted caddy was parked in the driveway. Doyle didn't go anywhere without that Cadillac.

Everything was locked so he broke the window in the back door and entered. Inside it was smoky and hot. The heat intensified with each step toward the front of the trailer. Along the way he quickly checked the bedrooms and bathroom but found no one. By the time he reached the living room he was coughing hard and was disoriented. He dropped to his hands and knees and flashing his kel light around the room, caught sight of Doyle Howland lying unconscious with empty booze bottles at his feet.

Jack threw Doyle over his shoulder and broke through the front door. Pouring the lifeless man on to the ground, Jack administered CPR until a coughing and vomiting Doyle Howland jerked back to life. He had to restrain Howland as he flailed away with his prosthetics. Doyle wore hooks for hands as reminders of Viet Nam. After Doyle regained consciousness, he spit and screamed and cursed Jack for saving his life.

"Goddamn you. Let me die. I want to die." He was silenced when the paramedics covered his mouth with an oxygen mask. Howland never thanked him for saving his life and half the cops gave him grief for saving such an asshole.

Doyle was universally disliked. All of the experiences the cops had with him were unpleasant at best. For thirty-five years Jack wondered if he had indeed done the right thing. Jack thought of all the assaults, burglaries, and general nastiness that would have been avoided if Doyle had gone up in smoke. But since he was

7

the "protect and serve" kind of cop, he guessed he had performed properly by saving the life of a genuine degenerate.

He spent his last day alone in his unmarked squad car. Jack took one more spin around the county in an official capacity. Near the end of the day, he answered a service call. As a detective, Jack usually let the assigned deputy perform that duty. But since he was in the area and knew the person requesting help, he volunteered for the call. Jack headed for the Graves farm along Stoney Lonesome Road.

Mattie Graves let him in the big warm kitchen. As usual, the old wood range kept the room cozy and the ever present coffee pot sat ready on the stove. Will Graves sat in his rocker between the tall kitchen window and the stove. Jack shook hands with the big man, but was not completely sure Will remembered him due to his dementia. Even though Will was old, he had a ham of a hand. Big, thick, wide and surprisingly soft and warm.

After some small talk, Mattie explained that she needed a light bulb changed in the pantry off the kitchen. Apologizing in her graceful dignified manner for calling the police over such a trivial matter, she explained that age and infirmity prevented her from performing the task.

"You don't need to apologize for that Mattie," Jack assured her. "Believe me, it's my pleasure."

After changing the bulb, he joined them at the kitchen table for a cup of rich, smooth coffee, known for its quality and quantity. Her mother-in-law had taught her how to make it on the wood stove when Mattie first came to the farm, cracking a raw egg into the grounds to cut the bitterness. Jack helped himself to a plate of homemade Christmas cookies.

He had known these people all of his life. Mattie had first taught him in elementary school and then later in high school English when she moved from a one room country school to Brunswick High. While growing up Jack had worked for Will on the farm and had stayed with them for several summers. They occupied a special place in Jack's heart. As he was leaving, Mattie pressed a small bag of cookies on him and extracted a promise that he would stop by for a drink over the holidays.

# CHAPTER THREE

M attie poured Will his first cup of coffee of the day. The black cast-iron range that dominated the kitchen was still the best way to make coffee she thought. But it took greater effort to make it that way these days. Although her movements were still graceful, age had imprinted stiffness and frailty upon them.

She poured hot side pork grease over homemade pancakes then liberally spread sugar on top of it all. She made Will's favorite breakfast knowing that it was unhealthy. But at his age he was entitled to indulge in one of the few remaining pleasures left to him. He ate in silence while Mattie sipped her coffee. Never much of a breakfast eater, she would have a little something later in the morning. Her husband's declining mental faculties and the grip of old age had left him with little to say.

Will returned to his rocking chair by the tall kitchen window near the stove. Arrayed on the wide sill were his tobacco cans, an assortment of worn pipes, magnifying glass, loose wooden toothpicks, and a small stack of unread Western novels.

Gazing out the kitchen window, Will rocked and puffed in time to the creaking of the chair. He was reduced to keeping watch as his sole useful purpose in life. Reaching to his left across his body with his big right hand, he tapped the ashes from the pipe into the grate on the range.

Mattie noticed the creaking had stopped in the corner and looked over to see that Will had drifted off to sleep again. That was about all he did anymore. Most of his days were reduced to the dream-filled slumber of an old man. She watched as Will drifted in and out of consciousness, mumbling about things that only made sense to him.

Still dressed in her night things, Mattie sat with her coffee at the kitchen table next to the stove. She needed the fire's warmth. Other than the shifting wood, the only other sound was the tick tock of the wall clock. Mattie wrapped her hands around the heavy white porcelain cup. Heat transferred from the hot coffee to her hands and acted as a temporary balm for an ever-present arthritic pain.

Tired out from the Christmas holiday, Mattie enjoyed the quiet and peace. This year had been more than her endurance could stand. It was simply too much for her anymore. And that strange flutter in her chest had returned.

On Christmas Eve, her granddaughter Anna had brought out the photo albums and induced Mattie to stroll with her down memory lane. Although Anna had heard the stories and the explanations many times, it was their yearly ritual. Their only granddaughter was working on her master's degree at the University of Wisconsin. The young woman reverted to a gangly, freckled faced, pigtailed, little girl at the sight of those photographs.

Mattie paged through the volume of old photographs and as she did so drifted back to those times. Mattie looked up from the photo album at the old man in the rocking chair and noted that he still had those big beautiful hands.

She thought back to 1943 and her senior year at the Brunswick Teachers College. Asked to the annual Masonic spring dance, her boyfriend Thomas Fitzgerald called at the appropriate hour and was met by her father. Fitzgerald came from a well-respected family of lawyers and politicians and Thomas was headed in the same direction. Judge Henry Beret and Gilbert Fitzgerald, Thomas' father, were Lodge brothers, former law partners, and friends. The two well connected families traveled in the same circles. Henry Beret was pleased with the thought that Thomas and Mattie would probably marry someday.

The dance, held at the Masonic Temple ballroom, welcomed servicemen on furlough and their friends. No drinking was allowed in the large basement ballroom, but that did not stop the participants from sneaking off to their cars for a nip. Uniformed servicemen milled around at the dance, usually more intoxicated than the general population. Although these young men were happy to be home, the wariness in their eyes could not be masked by gaiety or alcohol. None of them knew if this was the last time they would ever be home.

Dapper and agile, Fitzgerald expertly whirled Mattie around the dance floor to Glenn Miller's "In the Mood." His jet black tightly curled hair topped a tall athletic frame. Urbane and sophisticated, Fitzgerald was the most desirable bachelor suitable for marriage in Mattie's circle of friends. In the discussions he had with her father, the topic of marriage was enthusiastically encouraged. Thomas's dashing personality complimented Mattie's charming wit and intelligence. Mattie recognized that Thomas, or "Fitz," as he preferred to be called, was quite a catch.

As Mattie danced with Fitz in the center of the dance floor, a lone sailor in dress whites slipped in and took up space against the wall. He had his hands stuffed in his pockets and his sailor's cap was pushed low over his brow. She thought he looked familiar, but at first could not place him. There was something arresting about him, however, that drew her attention away from her dancing partner.

With the dance over, Fitz and Mattie made their way to a table near the sailor and Mattie recognized Will Graves instantly when their eyes met. They had not seen each other for many years, but Mattie remembered Will's steady gaze and wide shoulders. He had been fifteen years old when he delivered firewood to their home. She had been impressed with his maturity and confidence, maneuvering a huge team of horses and wagon around their woodshed, and the fact that he was an older boy.

On one occasion Will made his delivery just as Mattie and her friends were leaving the house to go skiing for the afternoon. Mattie, Fitz, her best friend Rebecca Moore and Rebecca's cousin Tippy Gamble passed him on his way into the driveway with the load of firewood. A few not so nice comments were made at Will's expense by Fitz and Rebecca. Mattie gave him an "I'm sorry" look, but he ignored her and them as he passed by.

An hour or so later, Mattie noticed Will's team of horses at the bottom of the ski hill and Will trudging up towards them at the top with a pair of skis over his broad shoulders. Not saying a word, he simply strapped on the skis and with numerous runs down the hill managed to make them all look like beginners. When he was finished he loaded the skis onto the wagon, climbed aboard and said "Gid up" as he lightly touched the reins to the horses' backs. She had gone to high school shortly after that and lost track of him, until he showed up at the dance.

Will Graves had grown into the man the boy had promised to be. When Mattie reintroduced herself to him, he commented that her friends had not improved much since the last time he saw her. He cut a self-assured figure in his uniform and Mattie was smitten.

The attraction was mutual, strong and true. Before Will shipped out again for the Pacific, they married. Their decision to marry had been rash, but mostly right in hindsight she thought. Nor was it an unusual action for 1943 in the midst of war. When she first walked into the kitchen of the Graves farm, her future father-in-law rose from the same rocker now slept in by Will and welcomed her into his home. She immediately knew that this place would play a huge role in her life.

Will informed Owen and Laura Graves that he wanted to marry Mattie before shipping out. Owen hugged her, shook his son's hand, and pronounced that they better get busy. There was no doubt of her certainty about marrying Will Graves and the loving arms of the Graves family reinforced her decision.

Will mumbled in his sleep causing Mattie to break from her daydream. She wondered what part of his life he was reliving in his dreams this time. He woke with a snort and looked around as if surprised. He said it was time to go outside and get some work done, but instead he went back to sleep. She hoped the dream was good.

# CHAPTER FOUR

Leaving her husband to his dreams, Mattie went upstairs to her bedroom and dressed for the day. The alcove just off her bedroom offered the best view of her backyard. For her, the alcove was the most peaceful spot on earth. As she looked out the window, she noticed how the snow clung to the clumps and rows of lilacs that she had planted in her backyard. Beyond its reaches she could see the courtyard and farm buildings. An empty space where the barn had once stood dominated. She would never forget the day it burned.

She had been summoned by Will that the barn was on fire. Within minutes the roadway, driveway, and yard were littered with cars, pickup trucks, and fire equipment. Fire hoses crisscrossed the courtyard of the farm as they tried to contain the fire from various angles. Nearby buildings were watered down to keep them from catching fire.

A wall of intense heat drove everyone back as the fire reached its zenith. Mattie watched the flames eat through the roof and melt the walls as the barn consumed itself. As the fire faded to embers and darkness descended upon the farm, everyone gradually left. Mattie went upstairs to change out of soot covered clothes. From the window of the alcove she saw him. Barely discernable in the darkness, leaning against the corner of the granary, hands stuffed in his pockets, Will stared into the coals, motionless, all alone. That was the end of the dairy farming and the beginning of the end of his life. Will Graves never recovered from the loss of his beloved barn.

Returning to the matters at hand, Mattie removed her cigarettes from the hidden compartment of her writing desk. She opened the window and lit her first one of the day. The air coming in through the window was cold enough to burn her nose. She liked how it felt.

Throughout her life, Mattie had written her thoughts in journals, poems, and letters. Lately, she had been working on a long letter to her granddaughter. After all, she had been a teacher and she saw no reason to quit her life's work just because she was no longer in the classroom. She had first taught eight grades in a one room country school. As the 1960's approached and country school consolidations occurred, Mattie moved to high school where she taught English until her retirement, after which she tutored.

Picking up where she had left off, Mattie continued her letter to Anna on a small sheet of monogrammed paper. Mattie settled into her task. Taking the pen into her aged hand, she composed herself first, then began to write. Although her penmanship was still beautiful, there was age in the flow.

"Anna, every life, indeed every marriage, has its disappointments and failed expectations. On the whole, my life with your grandfather has been positive and fulfilling. Whatever pain, sorrow, or regret has been worth the price of our life together. I just cannot believe how fast life has passed me by. Where did all that time go from when I married to now? It illustrates perfectly

Robert Frost's poem, "Nothing Gold Can Stay." All things in life, most especially the good things, are fleeting, just like a shooting star which streaks across the sky faster than you can formulate a wish, life begins and ends."

She paused from her writing and looked at the black and white framed photographs on the corner of her desk. The smallest was of John, her only child. He looked at the camera with skepticism and wariness. The look in his eye reminded Mattie of herself, but the rest was all his father.

Next to it sat a photograph taken on her wedding day. Will's confident gaze at the camera revealed his mature strength. Crisp and stark white, his uniform was worn with the bearing of a man who had earned the right. The image revealed strength. It was the core of the man she fell in love with and married.

In one stroke she had broken the yoke of her father's imperious heavy hand. She did the one thing that earned banishment from her father's life. According to her father, she married beneath herself. Not only was her husband a farmer, he was also Catholic. Even more disturbing to her father than that was the fact that he was a Democrat. She admitted to herself that the motivation to defy her father had been a part of the reason she married Will Graves; but only a part. The smallest part. Without the love and admiration she felt for Will, Mattie would never have married.

Her father was a stubborn and proud man. He decided that if it was her wish to marry this farm boy, then so be it. But she would do it on her own. Her father had not been present to give her away or dance at the party afterwards. His deep disappointment lasted a life time. He never got past the fact that the boy who had once delivered his wood married his only child. But Mattie Beret Graves did not apologize for her life. "Regrets are like ashes from a fire," she wrote Anna. "Simply the residue of life."

Will Graves and Mattie Beret were married under a beautiful old maple tree in the front yard at the farm on Stoney Lonesome

Road on a pretty spring day in May. Monsignor Brady officiated and Owen, Will's father, cleared a place in the hay mow for the dance. Laura, Will's mother, prepared a feast for the attendees. Two neighbors filled the evening with old time music. There were plenty of bottles passed around and at the end of the night the hat was passed to pay the musicians. She still pictured Owen leaning on a barn broom in the middle of the "dance" floor, draining the last few drops from a bottle of Christian Brothers Brandy.

Because there had been no time to get a wedding dress, she had worn the prettiest one she owned. Her mother, in absolute uncharacteristic defiance of her husband, had attended the wedding and dance. Mattie wore her grandmother's ring which served as a gift from her mother and as something old. Flush as the recent bloom of a flower, her reflection in the wedding photo was luminous. She had never felt better in her life than at that moment. Mattie believed that the promise of the photograph had been largely, if not completely, fulfilled. But, there was no denying the loss she always felt that her father had not been there to give her away.

She inhaled deeply. Every puff of every cigarette she had ever smoked made her feel like she was getting away with something. Mattie loved smoking in her alcove, alone. This was one thing that she could totally control. The one thing that was totally hers. While it was innocent enough to hide her smoking habit, she knew it revealed a deeper ability to deceive.

Returning to the kitchen once again, she found Will still asleep. Again this morning he had asked where their dog Truman had gone. He thought he had let him out, but Mattie gently reminded him that they had buried Truman a long time ago out in the back yard among the lilacs.

As she watched him sleep in his rocker, she wondered how much time he had left. Not long she thought. It was a good thing that he would probably go first. He would never be able to handle her death, be alone or take care of himself. He had been a wonderful husband. Although the scars of war and life had their effect, Will Graves had done admirably to meet all of her needs and accept her faults. His head was back against the rocker, still. It appeared that he was off on another journey.

# CHAPTER FIVE

After checking on Will who was still asleep in his chair, Mattie went back to her desk with coffee in hand. A small packet of letters shared space in the compartment with the Camel Straights. Sitting back in her chair she once again contemplated the past. She had a decision to make and soon, whether these letters should be given to Anna or burned. They concerned one of those loose strings in life that could not be tied. It had to be confronted or death would make the decision for her.

Rarely did she take the letters out anymore. She could recite them line by line. Normally, she just left the drawer open and gazed in as she thought and smoked. But she felt compelled to read them again.

The letters were sent to her by Thomas Fitzgerald following an accidental meeting at the county fair some years after her marriage to Will. The chance encounter sparked a longing Mattie had hidden from herself. The first letter simply said "I must see you again or I will die. Meet me at the place where we used to go on Saturday."

After sporadic rendezvous spread over several years, Mattie called it off. She explained at their last meeting that this clandestine life had to end, no longer willing to jeopardize her marriage. Fitz sent her the second letter after the last meeting. Mattie once again read,

"Mattie,

I am sure you think me awful for writing you against your wishes. But my torn and bloody heart will not let me rest. No poem could be written to describe the emptiness of my life without you. No musical note exists that is low enough to reach the depths of my despair. Life is meaningless without you.

I will agree to any terms you advance and promise that I will place no pressure upon you. Please open the door to your heart and save me. As Yeats said, 'I am looped in the loops of your hair.'

Eternally yours, _____."

Mattie relented and the resumption of the affair led to the birth of her son John. The affair continued for a while before she decided to end it. The goodbye was long and tearful but final. In the third letter, he accepted the state of things, pledged his undying love, and promised to forever watch for a sign that she had changed her mind, but she never did.

Will never said a word about any suspicions that he may have had. But when she became pregnant with John, Will moved out of their bedroom. He did not mention their inability to conceive. She told him one day that he should name the baby if it was a boy and she would do so if it was a girl. He agreed. A few days later he said quietly that he choose the name John, after his grandfather. When John was born, Will spent even more time in the barn.

Mattie never told a soul and Fitz was dead. The only link to this aspect of her life were the letters. She wondered how they would affect the lives of John and Anna. As she continued struggling with her dilemma, she was interrupted by a noise downstairs and quickly went to investigate, fearing that Will had fallen again. She found him on the porch floor with his barn clothes half-way on. He died with a smile on his face.

Although she couldn't have known, Mattie wouldn't have been surprised at his last thoughts. Will's final journey had been following Truman through the snow to the barn. God, it was beautiful outside he observed. A sky so blue and clear it almost hurt to look at it. And the barn, why, it looked new to him. Deep red, set off by white trim and a black roof, she stood as a monument to the life he'd lived. He stepped inside and closed the door behind him.

After the funeral, Anna moved in at Mattie's invitation. The flutter in her chest turned into a heart attack and a lengthy hospitalization. Her doctor said she was lucky to be alive considering her age, the severity of the attack, and the damage done.

No more stairs and no more cigarettes were the orders from the doctor. Although Mattie had never said anything before to anyone about her smoking, she felt it was necessary to tell her doctor. She instructed him not to reveal it to anyone else, anyway. The stair problem was overcome with a lift, but she simply ignored the no smoking ban.

Smoking at her desk in her alcove, Mattie made her decision. She added a post script to Anna's letter which she had completed upon her return from the hospital. After finishing it, Mattie carefully folded the letter and placed it on top of the three letters from Fitz in the bottom drawer with her cigarettes. She knew it would be found after her death. A wave of relief washed over her and she sat transfixed staring into the space for long moments before closing the drawer. She hoped for the best. A fresh May breeze carried the sweet fragrance of the lilacs into her room. It caressed her writing desk and ruffled the curtains.

A tiredness began in the deep recesses of her mind and spread outward across her entire body. Its suddenness and depth caused Mattie to forego her tea for a late afternoon nap. She barely had the strength to cross the alcove and lie on the bed. Mattie lay down on top of her bedspread after first removing her pillow from under its cover. Frail aged hands shakily removed her specs, folded and placed them on her night stand. Although it was warm, the breeze caused her to feel a chill so Mattie wearily pulled her favorite afghan over her as she allowed her body to sink into the bed.

Relaxing into the soft pillow she watched the shadows play on the wall and ceiling. The dying western light brushed the shadows from the big elm tree across her room. The soft rustle of the elm leaves serenaded her into a semiconscious dream state. Mattie loved her dreams. She plunged into deep sleep and her mind soared into places as if on a magic carpet ride. She would rise up to the surface of consciousness only to plunge again. She had always loved these little journeys. It freed her like a bird to swoop and dive and rise to swoop again.

For one last time, Mattie caught a ride on the May breeze and rode it out across the little valley swooping and diving and finally rising again.

# CHAPTER SIX

The death of Will Graves that winter surprised no one. Most everyone thought it a blessing that his heart gave out before he completely lost his mind. But Mattie's death that same year was unexpected. She had rarely been sick and only hospitalized to deliver her son. Everyone was shocked to hear of her heart attack and was relieved at her recovery. But shortly thereafter, her granddaughter found Mattie dead after apparently lying down for a nap. Jack had gone to the wake the night before and had stopped afterwards for a few beers.

In his half sleep Jack Delaney sensed Harry stirring beside him and did his best to avoid getting up to let him out. Never a fan of early morning, he was especially resistant after a late night. The reality of a cold wet nose in his ear, however, forced consciousness.

"Go lay down, dammit." Jack recoiled into his pillow turning away from his trusted pest. Not easily deterred, Harry thumped his big paw onto an exposed leg. His sharp nails caused further retort and recoil. An irritating cadenced bark, not unlike the perfectly timed drip.... drip.... drip.... drip.... from a faucet, produced the correct response. Jack let him out the back door.

Though small, the house had a roomy relaxed feel. Taking his coffee on the breezy screened in back porch he watched Harry make the rounds of the large fenced in back yard. It was not long before the Briard wanted in and wanted breakfast. Not for the first time did Jack wonder who ran the show.

He opened the paper and turned to the local arrest page recognizing a number of people listed. He noticed that Doyle Howland had once again made the paper. Disorderly conduct, again. Christ, Jack thought, why don't they just lock him up and leave him that way. He supposed, being a decorated, yet troubled Viet Nam vet, had its advantages. Still, it didn't change the fact that he always had been and would likely remain worthless. Jack mentally kicked his own ass again for saving the bastard's life.

There was plenty of time to mow the lawn next door before he had to get ready for Mattie's funeral. He took care of his little place and the landlady's next door as part of his rent. The arrangement had been satisfactory enough for him to remain in the same house for over twenty years. He finished his coffee and went outside to work on the lawn.

The brick Victorian style mansion next door dwarfed the small cottage he lived in. At one time, his place had been used as the guest house for the big place. Nestled among aged oaks, the two properties stood out in stark contrast in the once prestigious Third Ward of Brunswick. The university had worked its magic on the neighborhood and with few exceptions, most of the area now housed students. But because of Jack's ongoing efforts, the properties retained their original splendor. Even the Beret Mansion where Mattie Graves grew up, had been converted into a student rental and had become a shadow of its former stately self.

Jack had spent hours scraping, painting, fixing, repairing, replacing, trimming, mowing, planting and pruning. By rights, he should have had free rent and been paid for his work to boot. But, he couldn't squawk. The widow Fitzgerald had never once raised the rent. She didn't need the money. She just needed to be waited on.

"Mr. Delaney," Jack looked up from sweeping the walk after mowing the lawn, to see the widow behind the screen door and walked over.

"Good morning Mrs. Fitzgerald, how are you this morning?" Even though he had known the widow for nearly a quarter of a century, formality was in order. He thought of her always as the widow because of Rebecca Fitzgerald's constant reminder to everyone that she was indeed a widow. Jack had never known the prestigious Mr. Fitzgerald. His early death had given the missus her identity before Jack had moved in next door to a life of voluntary servitude.

"Would you be so kind as to drive me today?"

"Why I'd be honored ma'am," Jack replied.

"I'll be ready at 11:00 o'clock then." She retreated into the interior of her cavernous home with the assistance of her walker. Her vanity was such that she never used its help in public. For that, she required the arm of a gentleman.

He knew the widow would not be caught dead in his old pickup so he backed out her Deville and did a quick wash. Jack had no allusions about or desires for the widow's possessions or money. That is not why he stayed at the cottage and helped the old lady with the necessities of life. He liked her despite her iciness and he also loved the old place.

Even so, she took pains to remind him that her money, all of it, would go to the university to endow a chair in the political science department in honor of her beloved husband. On the way to the funeral, she returned to her favorite subject. "You know that the late Mr. Fitzgerald would have been a magnificent governor if his time had not been cut short," she said, telling him again about her husband's greatness.

"It is only fitting that a man of his stature be remembered and his good works be carried on," she added. She rarely deviated from her campaign to lionize him. "I have therefore employed Mr. Fitzgerald's former law firm to draft all necessary papers to put my wishes in place."

"Yes ma'am, sounds like a great idea." Jack could have cared less. He hated politics almost as much as he hated religion. Jack thought that hypocrisy was a central tenet of both, espousing fictionalized half-truths. Delaney's gritty realism left little room for mysticism and bullshit.

They took the highway south out of town for several miles before turning onto Stoney Lonesome Road which would eventually lead them to the church, ten miles away. Mrs. Fitzgerald had finally lapsed into a regal, welcomed, silence.

The tavern at the corner of the highway and Stoney Lonesome Road was closed for the funeral. The faded Walter's beer sign that hung on the pole announced Hank's Place. This was the bar Jack grew up in and lived above. It was the same place now owned and lived in by Cindy Robertson, his sometime girlfriend. Although Jack was glad that she was making a go of the place, she could have it, he thought. He'd had enough of the public.

Stoney Lonesome Road weaved narrowly through hills, around oak wood lots, and past farms. It carried Jack Delaney and Rebecca Moore Fitzgerald westward along its ten mile route. He especially liked driving along the road during this time of year. It was spring and as Jack drove along, he noticed that leaves had appeared as if by magic. The whispering pale green buds of yesterday had been transformed almost overnight to all variety of vibrant shades today. Everything was alive and seemed to be singing at the top of its lungs. It felt and looked like the entire countryside was making love to itself.

About half way down Stoney Lonesome Road, the gentle hills began to swell and the road topped out on a high ridge as it rounded the corner and descended into the little valley below. This was Jack's favorite view. Far down the valley where the road ran alongside Dismal Creek, stood the farm of Will and Mattie Graves. Before she had burned to the ground, the big red barn of Will Graves had been the eye's natural focal point.

The heavy Deville purred smoothly as it glided down the gentle slope into the valley. Glad for the silence afforded by the widow's reserve, Jack thought again about the day when the barn fire made this valley a sad place.

As they passed the Graves farm, Mrs. Fitzgerald broke her silence and observed that Mattie's lilacs were particularly beautiful this year. Groves and hedgerows of white and purple lilacs were in full bloom around the farmhouse. Their strong sweet fragrance engulfed the car as it passed by the farm.

"It's too bad that such a beautiful place has gone to ruin," she offered further. Jack had to agree. Will had let the place go after the fire consumed the barn and his years had progressed. Jack wondered what would happen to the place now that Mattie was gone. He was aware that her granddaughter Anna had temporarily moved in to take care of Mattie, but he had no idea if that would be permanent. He supposed that the developers were licking their chops at the prospect of carving up yet another farm for home sites. He wished that the Graves farm would not meet the same fate as so many other places along this road. But progress being what it was, Jack was not hopeful.

As they neared the end of Stoney Lonesome Road, St. Mary's Catholic Church came into sight with its white steeple and green doors shining brightly in the sun. Cars were beginning to drift into the parking lot and mourners were filing up the steps and into the church. The hearse bearing the remains of Mattie Graves was backed up to the side entrance.

# CHAPTER SEVEN

Jack sat next to the widow Fitzgerald near the front of the church. St. Mary's was packed with standing room only at the back of the church.

While it was true that Mattie Graves had outlived most of her contemporaries, she had friends from all ages. There had been no aging of the mind or spirit and certainly no disconnect from life. So Mattie had retained and continued to attain friends as her years advanced. Her oldest, dearest, and most complicated friend was taking up skeletal space on the red padded bench next to Jack Delaney.

He wondered what the widow could possibly be thinking about. Maybe she was reflecting on her long friendship with Mattie. Jack had lost count of the times he had brought the widow out to the farm to visit Mattie over the years. It had been his favorite duty in a long line of duties for the widow.

On those occasions, Jack would spend hours talking with Will Graves. Will would always bring out the brandy bottle and ask Jack if "he wanted a snort" which he always did. The two women would retire to the front room for their chat while Will and Jack talked farming and gossiped about neighbors. But a time came when they would sit for long periods just listening to the sound of the leaves. Never once in all the years before dementia did they talk about Sonny Howland's murder.

"How do we measure a life," Father Dan asked.

"Is it by the number of years on the calendar or the way one lives one's life? In Mattie Beret Graves' case, it was both. Her long and gracious life exemplified ...." And, as Father Dan spoke, Jack's mind wandered and he began to look around the room.

What remained of the Graves family was seated in the front right pew and from his vantage point he had a clear view of them. John Graves, the only son of Will and Mattie Graves sat with his bald head bowed over his tall narrow frame. His deeply tanned skin was testimony to all the years living in the Arizona desert. His wife had died two years before from breast cancer. Next to him sat their daughter Anna Graves McCucheon. All the bright light in the room seemed to shine upon her.

"We will now give those who would like to remember Mattie an opportunity to speak," and with that Father Dan sat down. The time had come for the memories and eulogies portion of the service. There began a procession of testimonials from those people whose lives Mattie Graves had touched and influenced.

When it came to his turn, Jack rose and made his way past the beautiful mahogany casket to the podium. It was a fairly safe assumption that Jack Delaney knew more people in the county than almost anyone else. Having grown up in a popular neighborhood bar and then spending thirty-five years on the Sheriff's Department had exposed him to scores of the neighborhood's good and bad citizens. He knew most of their secrets, good and bad.

"Mrs. Fitzgerald has asked me to read this to you on her behalf." Clearing his throat, he began.

'My dearest and oldest friend is gone. I have known Mattie Graves since she was a little girl when we grew up next to each other in the Third Ward. Just as she was for others, Mattie was my rock. There was nothing I couldn't tell her. She knew all of my secrets. All of them. And the nice thing about that, is once you asked Mattie to keep a matter confidential, she never, ever, betrayed you. We didn't always agree on things. And she certainly let me know it when she thought I was wrong. But it was her support even in trying times that I will always cherish. A person is lucky to have close friends. Most of us have only a few. Mattie had many. I only had one. She was always the prettiest girl at the dance. Her presence was always graceful and dignified. I loved her and will miss her for the rest of my days. I suspect my age will hasten our reunion. Goodbye for now old friend. I will see you soon. Signed, Rebecca.'"

With that Jack returned to his seat. As he did so, the widow patted his arm.

As the full choir of St. Mary's assured the congregation that Mattie Graves would be at peace in the valley, the pallbearers carried the casket to the hearse. The procession of cars following the hearse wound slowly back down Stoney Lonesome Road past the Graves farm to the top of the ridge. There they laid to rest the body of Mattie Beret Graves next to her husband in the cemetery on a pretty spring day in May. Will Graves had preceded her in death by five months.

Jack excused himself from the widow and left her in the car for a moment lost in her own thoughts. The immediate family lingered near the soon to be lowered casket. Most everyone else hastened their return to the church basement for a lunch provided by the ladies aide. There was sure to be Velveeta cheese on openfaced cream bread with crushed up potato chips sprinkled on top.

Ubiquitous at all funeral lunches were servings of Jello, cake, and mints. "Coffee or milk," a dutiful grandmotherly type would ask as you came to the end of the line.

He walked to the furthest corner of the cemetery at a point on the ridge directly above the Graves farm. The road leading off of Stoney Lonesome Road to the cemetery doubled back along the spine of the ridge so that the cemetery was literally on the bluff overlooking the buildings. It was there that Jack Delaney spoke the lines of Mattie Graves' favorite poem from memory. Mattie Graves taught that poem to every student she had ever had in and out of the classroom. He spoke the words in her honor. He spoke the words to Will Graves. He spoke the words to himself. He spoke the words to a life that no longer existed. Truly, nothing gold can stay.

# CHAPTER EIGHT

Harry loved patrol. The dog's long, coarse, black hair blew back from his eyes and face, perched on the front seat with his head out the passenger window. Several times a month Jack took Harry in his old truck and hit the road. Usually they headed out after the news for a couple of hours.

Retired, Jack no longer carried a gun. Nor did he have a scanner. Never had one. Listening to a police radio for thirty-five years had been enough. Armed with only his thoughts and the companionship of his big dog, Jack traversed the back roads of Brunswick County in a slow aimless drift.

The phone was off and in the glove compartment. He left law enforcement up to the people still toiling away in the trenches. But, old habits die hard and the need to keep an eye on things was now part of him. Even so, Jack stayed out of the way.

He knew nothing more pathetic than an old cop hanging around the station after retirement. The type without a life except as a lament about the good old days when cops were cops. They were dried up and spent after years and years of rubbing up against society's rougher edges. Their spirits were worn to a bloody stump. The marrow of their lives sucked dry by a thankless public.

Jack remembered the very first time he walked into the Brunswick Sheriff's Department to inquire about a job. In the middle of a conversation with the Sheriff about a law enforcement career, a crusty old veteran stepped into the office at the end of his shift. Deputy Odean Pedersen plunked his overflowing frame down onto the couch next to Jack in the small office of the Sheriff.

The dandruff from Odean's thick gray hair overflowed onto the shoulders of his worn brown uniform shirt. He didn't bother to brush it off. All manner of things graced a tie that had not seen a dry-cleaner's in a very long time. Coffee stains, cigarette ash, burn holes, and parts of leftover meals played up the length and across the breadth of his tie as it rose and descended over a doughnut swollen belly.

"This is Jack Delaney, Hank's kid," the Sheriff said by way of introduction to Odean. "He wants to be a cop."

Odean sat bolt upright in the chair from his previously slouched position. He snapped his head back and forth between the faces of Jack Delaney and the Sheriff several times with his mouth hanging open. Then he resumed his slouch. "The boy don't look like he's crazy," he said.

Odean drew exactly ten retirement checks before a lifetime of abuse and neglect collected its due. After spending ten months of retirement boring cops at the station, he went face first into his eggs one morning in the middle of another harangue about how crummy life had been. He was not missed. Jack swore he would never end up like Odean Pedersen.

Jack did his best to stay physically and emotionally healthy. No small task for a cop. Sooner or later, the ugly side of life that a cop sees has a way of filtering into and diluting the joy of life. But Jack had always stayed away from the Department and kept to himself when not at work. He tried to avoid the "us versus them" trap. "Us" being the cops and "them" being the public. A prevalent attitude in Copland. But no matter how hard he tried, hardness seeped in. His career was over and he was not about to hang around the Sheriff's Department.

Humid midsummer air flowed softly through the truck's cab carrying the sweet smell of fresh cut hay. He thought it to be the purest scent in all the world. But cutting hay did mean that you had to eventually bale it. Jack did not think that that part of haying was so sweet and was glad his haying days were long over.

Christ, he thought, he handled thousands of hay bales in the three summers he had worked for Will Graves. But it had been just the thing that was needed for a thirteen year old boy. His old man figured that a few summers working along side Will Graves would keep him busy and out of trouble.

John Graves, Will and Mattie's only son, had left home for college leaving Will in need of a hired hand. John boarded the bus the day after he graduated from high school. From that day until the death of Mattie Graves, John returned once a year. Only at Christmas. So Will hired Jack to work on the farm at Hank's suggestion.

The deal was struck one Saturday night at the bar. They were old friends and Hank knew that Will was short a hand. Young Jack was out dancing a waltz with pretty Cindy Robertson to a two piece old time band.

"So I hear young Johnny headed off for college," Hank said as he emptied an ashtray and opened up another bottle of Walter's Beer for Will.

"Yup," Will said. "He's gone." His voice did not betray how he felt about his son leaving home, but then he had never said anything one way or the other about his son. Those thoughts were kept to himself.

"What are you doing for help," Hank asked. "You can't do all that work alone."

"Hum, I suppose I'll have to hire somebody. Not sure who though. Hard to find a kid that knows how to work on a farm, you know," he said with a furrowed brow and shake of the head. Will took a swig of beer.

Hank pointed out to the dance floor towards his son. "What do you think of Jack," he asked. "He's a strong kid and a hard worker. Learns pretty fast too," he added. Will turned around and looked at Jack dancing with the Robertson girl.

"Well, hell, I don't know. Has he ever worked on a farm before?"

"No, but he's a quick learner and works hard," Hank said.

"Don't you need him around here?"

"Yeah, but I've had trouble with the boy lately. He's a good kid, but head strong. Don't know, maybe too much energy. Who the hell knows? My guts tell me that if somethin's not done it could become a problem."

"Girls, huh," Will chuckled. "Well, thanks I'll think about it. A little hard work never killed anybody."

"I couldn't agree more," said Hank. That sealed the deal.

On the first day, Will put him behind a flat sled known as a stone boat used to haul hay. Will would first load up two loads of hay on his wagons, then continue to bale the rest of the field by piling ten bales at a time onto the stone boat then slide them off in a stack. After they finished baling they ate supper and then milked the cows. After milking they unloaded the first two loads of hay baled in the day. After a hot shower he collapsed into bed where he remained motionless until 5:30 the next morning when Will shook him awake for another day in the field. He was very glad that his haying days were now over. Happy with the fragrance of the hay without the work.

Jack's aimless drift brought him to the west end of Stoney Lonesome Road. He eased the truck down into third gear and let the engine reduce his speed.

Jack turned east and passed St. Mary's Church. All was quiet and dark except for the rectory which emitted the faint flickering half-light of a television. He suspected that Father Dan was watching his girlie tapes again. It was from a burglary into the Rectory years ago that Jack had learned of the good Father's peccadillos.

Jack caught the burglar and got an admission regarding St. Mary's. The thief turned over a few tapes that he had taken from the Rectory. The burglar pled guilty to all of the charges so the evidence, which included the tapes, never made it before the public.

But Father Dan's heart was in the right place. He ministered to all, no matter who you were, with honesty, sincerity and love. Jack did not see the need to ruin a good man. He logged the tapes into evidence without specification. When Jack dropped off the recovered stolen items from the Rectory, he included them without comment. Being the good catholic that he was, Jack supposed the priest did much penance for his sins.

About a mile east of the church, the road made a sharp S turn down a steep gorge. Half way down the hill on the left hand side was a mailbox with "Howland" painted in black letters on the side of the box. Jack looked for Doyle Howland's rusted Caddy but it was gone and the place was dark. It was too early for him to be home, at any rate. It was only midnight and Doyle would be half way into a drunk at some watering hole around the county. If it was later in the night Doyle's car would be parked next to some gal that he had drug home.

He could not see why women went out with the man. Maybe it was the fact that he had two hooks instead of hands. Maybe his disabled vet status granted him the favors of the ladies, Jack speculated. He supposed the man was entitled to some special treatment even if he couldn't stand him. After all, he had given both of his hands for his country in a cause that could not be justified. Doyle would never feel the soft touch of a woman's body on his fingertips ever again. A high price indeed for service to his country, Jack thought.

He crossed the narrow bridge and began the ascent up the other side of the gorge. He reached out and scratched Harry's ears. "Well old boy, what do ya say we call it a night and head home?" Harry licked his hand and stuck his head back out the window. He was happy no matter what Jack proposed.

Driving past the Graves farm, he saw the lights on and Anna's little car parked by the garage. Word was that Anna had stayed on for the last few months after Mattie's death to clean up the estate. John left for Arizona when the first clod of dirt thumped on the top of Mattie Graves' mahogany casket. He had given all he was going to give to Stoney Lonesome Road and its people. John's life was elsewhere and he was gone.

Before the funeral he signed papers at the lawyer's office that he wanted nothing to do with the farm and that Anna was to receive everything that came from his mother's estate. Jack could never figure out John Graves' hatred for this place. But he supposed it had something to do with the murder of Sonny Howland and the taint of suspicion against Will. He didn't know how it all fit, but that was the only thing that made any sense.

As Jack wound his way home he thought about the murder of Sonny Howland, Doyle's father. Sonny proudly carried the mantle of family bully, but he did so with a certain amount of charm. Good looks, charm, and danger drew women of all types to him.

Sonny took part in many fights out in the parking lot behind Hank's Place. He was big, tough, and liked to sucker punch. If he got someone down on the ground he put the boots to them. He was a tough son-of-a-bitch. There was no better place to act tough than in a neighborhood country bar on a Saturday night when all the folks were gathered to dance. Although he had been thrown out many times for fighting, Hank always let him back in after a grace period. He would behave himself for a while, chastised like a disciplined child. But just like a loose bull in the pasture, Sonny could not be trusted. Sooner or later, the bully in him would rise up and Sonny would lash out.

On one particular Saturday night in August of 1950 such a fight occurred. Mattie and Will had just come in off the dance floor after a set of waltzes. When Mattie and Will danced, people watched. They were poetry in motion as they went around and around and around to the rhythmic one, two, three, one, two, three of the music.

That particular night, Sonny was pretty lit up. As Will and Mattie walked by he leaned towards them and said something. Will spun around and hit Sonny Howland square in the nose with all of his might and the fight was on. After busting the place up and nearly killing each other the fight only came to an end when Mattie crashed a beer bottle over the top of Sonny Howland's head, knocking him out. Three weeks later he was found shot to death in a remote part of the county.

There was bad blood between the Howlands and the Graves that went back a long ways. Add Sonny's offensive comment together with the ensuing fight, and the authorities focused on Will as a likely suspect. Mattie swore that Will was home with her at the time the murder was pin pointed. Because her family name carried a lot of weight in Brunswick, the authorities backed off. The murder was never solved.

When Jack reached the top of the ridge by Cemetery Road he felt a cold chill. Shrugging it off he reached over and scratched Harry for good luck. The big dog always made him feel better.

# CHAPTER NINE

B eing able to light a cigarette with a set of hooks instead of hands was the first thing Doyle Howland learned to do after Viet Nam. It had taken him over a year to master the task, but he no longer marveled at his ability to do so. Extracting a pack of Pall Malls from the paper carton on the front seat next to him, Doyle deliberately tore off the cellophane and opened the top. Removing exactly one unfiltered cigarette, he placed it in his mouth with his right hook.

With continued precision Doyle proceeded next to a book of matches. Holding the book in the grasp of one hook, he removed one match and struck it to life with the other. The brief intense flair illuminated a face that had known little pardon. The discarded match joined others on the floorboard of the old rusted out Cadillac where they mixed with cigarette butts and empty booze bottles. Life's pain had squeezed the vitality from Doyle's worn face.

He sought relief from the pain in a bottle of booze. It took a lot of liquor to dim his hatred and anger. But unless the effort resulted in blackness, the pain never went away. At the core of his hatred was the name Graves.

From his vantage point at the back of the Brunswick Cemetery, he had a clear view of the Graves farm on Stoney Lonesome Road below him. He watched as Jack Delaney's tail lights went out of view at the top of the ridge. For a moment, Doyle watched to see if the cop would check out the cemetery, but no car lights appeared. Doyle frequently saw the pickup wandering all over the county. He blew the smoke past nicotine stained teeth and cracked lips onto the grimy windshield. Hank Williams' aching sadness played softly on the tape deck. Hank Williams gave voice to loneliness and despair, music Doyle knew by heart.

Dropping the spent cigarette butt into a stale beer can, Doyle got out of the car and stumbled over to the Graves family plot. He looked down at Will's headstone and swore.

"You killed my daddy you son-of-a-bitch."

Doyle stumbled across the cemetery to a forgotten plot adorned by a central headstone with "Howland" inscribed upon it. There in the darkness he located his father's grave. Dropping to his knees he rubbed the name clear with the sleeve of his shirt.

Walter "Sonny" Howland
Born April 1, 1918
Died August 21, 1950

With Sonny dead the family was reduced to public assistance at a time when that mattered. Doyle doubled over and sobbed into the grass. "I swear I'll get even Daddy. I swear it on your grave. I'll get those cocksuckers if it's the last thing I ever do."

He must have passed out because an irritating buzz in his ear woke him up. "Fucking mosquitoes," he swiped at his ear ineffectually with his hook.

Once again taking up his observation post in his car, he watched Anna come out of the house and get into her car. "Yup" he thought, just like clock work. Three a.m. Every night at this time she drove into the Brunswick Coffee Shop. He didn't know what the fuck she was up to, nor did he care. Doyle was merely interested in the pattern. As he had with Delaney, he watched her tail lights recede up Stoney Lonesome Road and disappear around the bend at the top of the ridge.

Noting the lightning far off in the western sky, he took a long pull on the bottle and lit another cigarette, thinking about his old man.

For all his faults, Sonny took his kid everywhere. Little Doyle spent the greater part of his first couple of years in a tavern watching grown men getting drunk.

He watched from atop the bar at Hank's Place one night while his old man laid out three guys, one, two, three. Afterwards, he told him, "There is nothin' to fightin' kid. Hit 'em as fast and as hard as you can until they stop movin'." Doyle never forgot the lesson.

Fighting had always made Doyle feel like a man. To beat another man into submission with the raw power of his fists had given Doyle a feeling of completeness he had found nowhere else. He had thought many times how he wished he had lost his jewels instead of his hands. There had been no poundings given by Doyle Howland since his fists had been blown into unrecognizable stumps. God, he missed his hands.

Before they were gone, Doyle could do anything with them. He had excelled in shop and his projects had been the hallmark of the class. He had that certain touch and feel that is the natural gift of a man who can work with his hands. His projects were polished in a way that other high school productions simply could not match.

These skills paved the way into the Army in spite of a checkered past. His brushes with the law were overlooked as minor in comparison with the potential he offered the United States Army.

Once in, he welded, machined, and fabricated his way up the ladder to sergeant and head of the machine shop. This was indeed a lofty position to attain for a Howland. While stationed in Viet Nam a welding explosion took away his only means of distinction and cut short what was turning out to be a career in the Army. Doyle looked down at his hooks in disgust, then returned to the current mission.

Finishing off a pint of Jack Daniel's he dropped his spent cigarette butt into the empty bottle and tossed it onto the floorboard of the car. As he drove to the Graves farm he estimated that he had one hour before her return.

With his car hidden on the side of the machine shed away from the road, he walked on the gravel driveway so as to avoid leaving tracks. This was not his first experience at casing a joint. He slipped off his shoes on the front steps so that he would not leave any dirt in the house. Then he slipped onto the porch in his stocking feet.

The low light of the kitchen revealed a large high ceilinged room. He saw right off that it was pretty messy. Loose papers, magazines, and books were arrayed in no particular way on the large oak table that was the room's centerpiece. To his left was a rocking chair sandwiched between a tall window and an old black cook stove. To the side of the stove was a sink full of dirty dishes. Lazy bitch, he thought. If she lived with him she would wash the fucking dishes.

Off to his right was an open door and it was here that he began his reconnoiter of the house. The room appeared to Doyle to be some kind of an office. Files, papers, and marked boxes were arrayed haphazardly on the shelves. A small black trash can was overflowing with crinkled up paper. Some of it falling onto the floor. A small desk had been placed up against the window. He marked this room in his memory. It was a good place to start the fire.

Doyle moved upstairs. He looked, snooped, prodded and poked his way around from room to room taking in the sights and smells of his enemy. Doyle was careful not to disturb anything. That did not prevent him from stealing a little something, however. He couldn't help himself. It was a way to count coup against a sworn enemy.

The kitchen clock announced that it was time to go. Standing in the doorway of Anna's room he breathed in her smells. Leaning over he sniffed at her perfume bottles arrayed haphazardly on the top of the dresser. Smiling to himself he thought maybe he would add a little pleasure to his final plan if circumstances permitted. Doyle bent over the unmade bed and breathed deeply from the pillows without touching them.

Leaving the upstairs, Doyle quickly explored the remaining rooms on the first floor. Just off the kitchen was a large formal dining room and next to it a front parlor. This last room was the most fancy and unused. Stiff formal furniture sat in the dusty silence. Large oval pictures of long dead relatives hung in ornate frames on the walls.

He left the same way he came, turning right out of the driveway towards his place. He had all the information he needed to execute his plan.

# CHAPTER TEN

Jack drove and thought his way through the changing seasons. Foggy summer nights cooled into crisp autumn days which then gave way to the long cold hand of winter.

His return to the Graves farm was the first in a long time. Word had filtered through to Anna that Jack was a handy man. Her request that he help her with a repair job prompted the current visit. An early winter ice storm had caused damage to the roof. Jack loaded his tools and his dog into his truck and drove out to the farm on a clear cold morning to make the repairs.

It was the first time he had seen Anna since the funeral the previous spring. He knew she had been living at the farm by the presence of her car and the lights on in the house late at night. He was also aware of her nocturnal habit of frequenting the café. Except briefly at the funeral, he had not actually spoken to her for many years. He remembered Anna as a kid, not the grown woman who stood before him in the doorway of the porch.

"Mr. Delaney, thank you for coming out so soon," she said as she came down the steps and extended her hand.

Accepting her hand with a nod he managed a "my pleasure ma'am. Please call me Jack."

"I really don't know what I would have done. The man at the garage told me you sometimes do repair work. I was glad to call someone I knew."

They went around to the back of the house. A branch from the huge white pine, covered with snow and ice, had broken off and poked a hole in the corner of the roof. Although it was quite a mess, Jack figured he would be able to clean things up and fix the roof in one day.

"Say, while I'm here, would it be alright for my dog to roam around," he asked, pointing toward the cab of his faded blue truck. Anna followed the direction of his hand and there was Harry with his big head out the window looking at them. "Of course. Please let him out. He's a Briard. Just like Gramps' old dog."

"Sure is. Ever since I worked for your grandpa I have liked them. They are great dogs." By this time the two of them were talking to and petting the animal as he strained towards them through the window with his big tail thumping the back of the seat.

"Come on Harry." Jack opened the door and an ecstatic Harry bounded out into the snow.

"My God, he's beautiful."

"Goofy mutt. He loves the snow. Just loves it. One thing about having a Briard, you are never lonely. Wherever you are - they are there - velcro dogs," Jack offered as he playfully kicked snow at Harry who was running around as if he had never seen snow in his life.

"I named him after your grandpa's Briard, Truman. Will told me he named Truman after President Harry Truman. So I named Harry in their honor."

"I remember Gramps talking about Harry Truman," she recalled. "He was his favorite president."

Harry settled down, Anna went back into the house, and Jack got to work. He went about his task in his usual careful methodical way, not unlike his approach to solving a case. Before he brought out the tools, he sized up the job and formulated a plan to carry it out. About half way through the morning Jack felt the absence of Harry. Stopping his work he called for him, but did not get the usual bounding response.

After a quick search he realized that Harry must be in the house because there was no way he would run off. His inquiry was treated by apologies from Anna and licks from Harry.

"Oh, I hope it was okay to bring him in. He looked like he needed a treat. I am sorry if I shouldn't have," Anna apologized as Harry stood beside her, tail wagging.

"No, no, that's perfectly alright. He is a shameless beggar on top of being a shameless flirt." Jack scratched Harry's ears and smiled at Anna. He could not help but notice the warmth of the kitchen and the smell of the coffee. Apparently reading his mind Anna brightened and asked, "Would you like to come in for a cup of coffee? You look like you could use a break."

"Sure. That would be very nice."

Leaving his heavy snow and sawdust covered outer clothing on the porch, Jack entered the warm kitchen in his stocking feet.

"I see you use the old stove."

"Absolutely. I love it. Every time I use it I think of Grams," she said as she poured steaming coffee from the pot on the stove. "Take anything in it?"

"No thanks, black is just fine." Carefully sipping the hot liquid, he thought about how long it had been since he had coffee this good. "You have inherited Mattie's knack for brewing coffee on the stove."

"Thank you. She told me that my great-grandmother taught her how to make it when she came to the farm." By this time,

Harry had gone to sleep lying on Jack's feet. Jack wiggled his toes under the big dog connecting with Harry in a quiet sort of way.

"Your grandmother taught me *Nothing Gold Can Stay* in my high school English class. She always talked about that poem, and it's the only poem I know by heart," Jack said.

"It was her absolute favorite poem," Anna agreed.

This launched them into a discussion of Mattie Graves and the role she played in each of their lives. They remembered that Mattie taught them the way a poem should be written. How Frost had said a poem should begin in delight and end in wisdom. Their shared understanding of his poetry was a reflection of Mattie's impact upon them.

"WOOF!!!!" Harry lurched to a standing position and barked at the same time. Both Anna and Jack nearly jumped out of their skins as Harry barked again.

"Quiet," Jack said firmly. "Sorry about that. What can I say, he is a Briard. It's just what they do." Jack, reminded by the time, excused himself.

He was unable to finish his work before dark, which came early in winter. Upon retrieving Harry from the house Jack apologized for having to come back a second day. He was pleased that Anna acted happy at the prospect.

As he drove away from the farm, he watched Anna in his rear view mirror retrieve the mail from the mailbox then, look up and wave. Jack eased out the clutch and leaned back into the seat a content man.

# CHAPTER ELEVEN

It was nearly dark by the time Jack got to the corner of Stoney Lonesome Road and the highway. On impulse, he turned into the parking lot of Hank's Place. There were a few cars parked up near the building. Not many out tonight, he thought.

Cindy Robertson was tending bar as usual. Since buying Hank's Place, her days off had been few. Her business was in the black, but it took everything she had to keep it from slipping into the red.

"Hey good looking," she greeted him with a smile as she reached into a cooler to retrieve a Leinie's for him.

"Hi Cin," he said as he returned her smile and took a long pull from the bottle. Jack greeted the others at the bar by name. Everyone returned the greeting with friendliness and warmth. No one was seated at the tables and the lights were turned low in that area. The kitchen was dark. Only the long narrow bar area was adequately lit, a few patrons were huddled near the elbow in the bar where they could converse and watch TV. Jack sat apart from them down the bar.

"What's new," she asked.

"Same old stuff. Been working out at the Graves place fixing the roof."

"Oh yeah, I hear Mattie's granddaughter has taken up permanent residence," she said. "But hasn't been in here though. Seems more like the coffee shop type to me."

"Nice girl."

"Girl. Every woman is a girl to you. She must be in her thirties at least."

"Like I said. Girl."

Jack slid the empty bottle to the edge of the bar. She replaced it with a full one. Jack glanced over his shoulder towards the kitchen. "Kitchen's closed, huh? I was hoping to avoid cooking dinner tonight. Getting old I guess. Tired out."

"Well you are right on both counts. The kitchen is closed and you are getting old. But, I can make you a pizza."

"That will do."

"Pepperoni," she asked.

"Why change now?"

Jack watched Cindy serve the other customers and then take his frozen pizza from the freezer and place it in the pizza oven. If she wasn't the sweetest girl he had ever known, there was none to be found. Fifty years of life had not stolen that away.

She had never married and there had never been any kids. Up until her bar purchase, Cindy had worked hard at whatever work was available in and around Brunswick. Always pleasant, she never complained. They had known each other since grade school at Maple Drive. The one room school with eight grades had been presided over by Mattie Graves.

They mixed together the way most country kids did back in the early 1960's. There was school, sliding, skiing and skating parties. The occasional 4H dance and other neighborhood events where they got together. But their crossing had an added dimension. Cindy's parents frequented Hank's Place. So nearly every

Saturday night while growing up he and Cindy could be found waltzing around the dance floor. He thought about those times as he watched her movements. They were familiar to him in that way of people who have known each other for a very long time.

They shared the pizza and the game they had come to play. She wouldn't take anything for the beer and pizza. Jack always left a tip that more than generously covered what he owed.

Jack first noticed that Cindy's older brother Herb was about to play a song by the soft tuning of his worn guitar. He carried the guitar around with him from bar to bar often without ever playing a thing. Then out of the blue he would play and sing something soft and easy, mostly sad. The years had reduced Herb's range, but he was still pretty good even though he missed a few high notes now and then.

After listening to the song, Jack bid Cindy goodnight. He eased his truck out onto the highway. Smoothly and slowly Jack unlimbered the cold engine until it purred along at 50 mph. He had to take it easy on the old girl. She couldn't quite hit the high notes anymore, either. It seemed like a Robert Frost kind of a day. It began in delight and ended in wisdom.

# CHAPTER TWELVE

Anna had converted the pantry off the large kitchen to serve as a writing space. Although she had tried to work in Mattie's alcove, her grandmother's lingering presence stymied her efforts. The pantry suited her needs better and was a familiar comforting spot.

As a child, Anna played in the pantry while Mattie worked in the kitchen. A tall window brightened the small room. Evenly spaced shelves lined both sides of the room bracketing the window. It was there that she placed Mattie's writing desk in between the rows of shelves. Although the room was not large, the high ceiling, open doorway, and tall window lent an easy feel to the surroundings. Sitting now at the desk Anna looked out onto the snow covered side yard of the house.

She was surprised by her disappointment that Jack had called to postpone his return to finish his work. Anna had looked forward to seeing him and Harry this morning. Mrs. Fitzgerald had apparently fallen and Jack was needed today for her care. He promised to return soon, probably tomorrow.

It had been a very long time since any man had stirred feelings inside of her. A long childless bad marriage had left her sour on men. Her divorce had allowed her a rebirth in spirit and liberty that Anna protected with conviction.

Madison had been the perfect place to begin her new life. Two years before her move to the farm she had been accepted into the English master's degree program. Those years had been spent soaking up the libertine ambiance of Wisconsin's capitol city. It had been a great time generally without worry or responsibility except for herself and her studies.

Now, suddenly without warning, there was this man and his dog putting the faint glimmerings of a smile in her heart. Anna's intuition, usually keen, told her that the vibes given off by Jack Delaney were good ones. Any man with the type of relationship he had with his big dog had to be decent and kind.

With a fair amount of guilt, she ignored her thesis which had been placed on the top shelf out of sight. Instead she worked on her journal. For now, she put down her pen and looked out the window at a beautiful clear blue sky amplifying the beauty of the pristine snow. Mattie always liked to say that snow covered up all imperfections. The morning sunshine shown on the desk and beckoned her outside.

Walking down the field road behind the buildings towards the woods made Anna think of her grandfather. He would often take her on walks or rides on the tractor around the farm. She walked along the snow covered road from the field into the woods.

Dismal Creek passed through the corner of the Graves property. It ran across the path of the road near the edge of the woods. Her grandfather's small wooden bridge had long ago rotted out and was mostly washed away by rains and neglect. Anna gingerly stepped onto the remains of the bridge and a rock or two to get across the shallow narrow creek. Her movements were not unlike the swift motion of a checker player's hand in a triple jump move.

The snow covered woods stood silent. Pine trees and large oak tree branches were covered thick with snow. Rabbit and deer tracks broke the snow ahead of her on the road.

She brushed the snow off a large stump and sat down for a few minutes. Although alone in the large woods, Anna felt no loneliness. The low winter trajectory of the sun across the sky allowed the color blue to dominate overhead and provided a brilliant background to the snow and dark shapes of the trees.

Once again taking up Will's walking stick, Anna resumed her stroll along the narrow snow covered field road. Her grandfather's handmade stick was worn smooth by his use. "WG" was carved near the top of the stick. Her grandfather had used it for many years on his daily walks around the farm. She imagined his big beautiful, surprisingly soft, warm hands wearing the stick to its polished smoothness by long use. For as big of a man as he had been, her grandfather had been surprisingly gentle.

As Anna wandered along the lane through the snow laden woods, she began to puzzle again about the letter from her grandmother. The long and gracious letter from Mattie to her had been found not long after the funeral. There were lessons and observations to ponder for many years to come.

But the postscript puzzled Anna. Her thoughts of the letter caused her to shorten her walk and return to the house. Returning to the writing desk Anna once again read her grandmother's final words. Postscript.

Anna, I have long wondered what to do with a certain piece of information that I possess. My reluctance in revealing its nature to you or your father has been part self-preservation, part loyalty and part concern for your welfare.

However since that which I alone possess impacts your life in a significant way, I have decided to bequeath my knowledge about the subject to you.

Attached to this letter are three more written to me at periods of great confusion and pain in my life. They tell a story about your grandparents never before revealed or known to anyone outside of those who participated. For many many years I thought of destroying the evidence of this past episode, but in the end decided to make them part of my legacy to you, such as it is.

By the time you read these words I shall be gone. All of the other participants in this episode are also dead. I will do no more than give them to you without further comment. They speak for themselves. In doing so, I will have kept a promise to myself and to the others never to reveal the secret by my own hand. It is someone else's hand and words that will tell the story. No one else knows.

My dear sweet Anna these are the last words I shall ever write. When I close this letter my pen will be forever still. Whether I live one minute more or linger for a number of years, I have said all that I have to say. From now until I rest, my thoughts will be mine alone.

Love, Your Grandmother.

Mattie had written the p.s. the afternoon she passed by the date and time noted at the top of the page.

Apparently, she had laid down for her usual afternoon nap after writing the final goodbye because Anna found her covered and peaceful on her bed in the last light of day. When she had gone to her room to check on her, she found her relaxed in death. Mattie's gold rimmed glasses were folded neatly on the night stand. Anna sat next to her for long moments until the sky darkened black and the only light came through the partially opened door from the hallway lamp. Anna's soft crying was the only sound in the house except for the ticking of the wall clock in the kitchen down stairs.

But, what on earth had happened to the letters? They were simply nowhere to be found. Anna had searched high and low in every nook and cranny but to no avail.

She even had checked with her grandmother's attorney, but had received no help at all. He was very clear that to his knowledge no such letters existed.

Her call to her father had likewise yielded similar negative results. When pressed, he had asked why would I care about a couple of old letters anyway.

"Remember our deal," he asked.

"Yes, I remember."

"So ask me anything you want, you know I'm sworn to tell you the truth."

"Alright Dad this counts, do you know anything at all about these letters," she asked.

"No," he answered emphatically. "Now are you satisfied."

"Okay, okay."

She concluded that her dad had no knowledge of the letters because of their pact. When asked a direct question from each other "that counted", they had sworn to always tell each other the truth. If he said he didn't know, he didn't know. That was that.

The only explanation was that Mattie had changed her mind and destroyed them in a last minute change of heart. It seemed to be the only plausible thing that could have occurred. But she could not let it go. Somehow she needed to find out what was in those letters. Maybe Jack could help. After all, he had been a policeman for many years. Anna resolved to bring this up with him at the next opportunity.

# CHAPTER THIRTEEN

Three days passed before Jack was able to return and finish work on the house. His day began and ended with no sight of Anna. Her car was gone and the lights were off inside. With clean up complete and the dog loaded in the front seat of the truck, he let the engine warm for a few minutes. As they sat idling Anna returned from wherever she had been. After a friendly greeting, Jack apologized for his long absence and inability to fix the house until today.

"The widow broke her hip in a fall," he explained as his voice caught. "She is not good."

"Is she going to be alright," Anna asked.

Jack looked at his feet and shook his head. Tears ran down his cheeks. "Sorry," he said as he wiped away the tears. "Don't know where that came from."

Anna reached out and put her hand on his shoulder giving it a squeeze. "That's okay. You must care for Mrs. Fitzgerald a great deal."

"Yeah, I guess I do. Known her forever, you know. They did surgery on it, but she'll never walk again. Probably won't live, it's sad," he rambled. "Must be hell to get old."

"He must give you comfort," Anna gestured with her chin towards the truck and the big dog.

"Sure does. Harry is all heart."

"Hey, how about joining me for dinner? Nothing fancy. Linguine and marinara sauce. Salad. Bread." He gladly accepted.

Jack built a fire in the old black cook stove, while Anna talked of her trip to Madison. The English Department was becoming impatient waiting for her thesis to be completed. She had delivered her unfinished rough draft to them in an attempt to buy a little time. A grudging extension of one year was granted on the sole grounds that the work delivered was superb. No slack was given for her personal troubles or tragedies, however. Such was the academic life.

"For a very long time all I ever wanted to do was get my master's, teach, and work on my Ph.D. Dr. McCucheon, English Professor. Now it seems hollow, trivial."

She went about preparing the dinner. At her request Jack opened a bottle of red wine she had picked up in Mad Town. After getting everything ready for dinner, Anna lit incense around the house and then excused herself for a few minutes.

Jack watched as Anna disappeared up the steps. From his vantage point at the table, Jack surveyed the kitchen. He noticed that Will's rocking chair was still in its place and that his things remained on the windowsill. As he looked around Jack could see that the place was in serious need of paint. The old house was sound, but badly needed attention. He also noticed that Anna was not the best housekeeper in the world. Books, magazines, and newspapers were piled and scattered everywhere.

Anna closed the door to her room at the end of the hall. She opened the window, lit some incense and took a deep drag on the joint she had managed to get while in Madison. Anna quickly changed clothes, splashed on some perfume, and returned to the kitchen. She found Jack looking into the pantry as she descended the stairs.

"Find anything interesting," she teased.

"Ah, just checking out the place. Didn't mean to be nosey." Embarrassed, he returned to his chair by the table.

They ate and talked. She sure seemed chatty all of a sudden. He also noticed she ate like a horse and wondered how anyone who ate that much could look so good. As they sipped the wine they munched on chocolates Anna bought on State Street in Madison. Anna had drawn her curly auburn hair into a ponytail. Her deep, wide set green eyes peered out over her freckled high cheekbones to look right through him. Jack was captivated by her.

"I have been meaning to ask you something," she said. "How well did you know my grandparents?"

"Known them all my life. We were neighbors and they came to the bar a lot. And I worked for Will, of course. Mattie was my teacher. Yeah, I'd say I knew them both pretty good."

He poured the last drop of wine into her extended glass. "Oops, time for another bottle," she laughed and pulled out a merlot from her shopping bag. Jack obliged opening and pouring the musky liquid into their glasses.

"So why do you ask," he said.

"Well, I've got a mystery to solve and I thought that your detective skills and knowledge of my grandparents would be helpful."

"Sure, be glad to help. What have you got," he said leaning back in his chair, cradling his glass of wine.

"I've got this ....." as she began, Jack sat up and blurted. "Oh, my God! I forgot to call the widow. I have to call her. Would you mind if we took a short break. I am sorry. I don't mean to interrupt, but she really counts on me stopping or calling everyday. I mean every day."

Anna excused herself and went upstairs while Jack phoned the widow.

"Hello," a very weak and shaky voice came on the line after being screened by the nurse.

"Mrs. Fitzgerald," he said. "It's Jack. Sorry for calling so late, but I got hung up."

"I was beginning to wonder if I would hear from you today. You know how much I look forward to hearing your voice," she whispered.

"How are you tonight?"

"Oh, the same old cripple. My hip is very painful."

"Are they giving you enough pain medication?"

"They are always giving me something. No one listens to me. They don't know anything," she complained.

"You get your rest. I'll be by tomorrow to see you," Jack promised.

"Okay, thank you for calling."

"You rest easy now. Good night."

"Good night." Jack hung up the phone.

Anna had made another pass at the joint and was now seated at the top of the stairs eavesdropping on Jack talking to Mrs. Fitzgerald. She smiled at the care and concern in his voice and the kind way he spoke with her. She thought it was sweet. Anna returned to the kitchen as he hung up the phone.

"All tucked in," she asked.

"Yeah," he said with a shake of his head.

Jack opened the fire gate and fed in a few small chunks of wood. They settled once again into the chairs at the table. Resuming their previous conversation, Anna filled Jack in on her grandmother's message to her and the perplexing mystery of the misplaced letters. But, as she explained to Jack, the true mystery was the secret contained in them.

"What on earth could it be about," Anna wondered.

"Must be the murder," he offered with some certainty. "Can't be anything else."

"Murder. What murder?"

"Will was accused of killing a man. It was never proven, dropped. But it wasn't solved either," Jack explained.

"My grandfather? Gramps? "

Jack told Anna about how Will Graves was accused of killing Sonny Howland. He explained the long held hatred between the Howlands and the Graves, the long ago fight between their fathers, the fight between them at the bar, and Sonny's death.

"Honest to God. I have looked at this case many times. Could never figure it out. But everyone thought Will killed him. I never did."

Anna was struck numb with shock and disbelief. She kept repeating that "Gramps was so gentle," not believing that he could ever do such a thing.

"I think there was more to Will Graves than most people think. Have you ever looked into the Presidential citation he received in World War II? The one that was shown at his funeral."

"No, not really, I never gave it much thought I guess."

"Well, I did. Would you like to hear it," he asked.

"Of course."

"Will was a seaman aboard a sub patrolling the waters along the Equator. In an effort to get information, the Navy ordered them to sink a boat and capture a prisoner. They torpedoed a large Japanese ship. The sub came up to capture their prisoner. A line was thrown out into the water and a sailor was hoisted aboard. Your grandfather was ordered to shoot any sailor trying to climb aboard. According to the report he poured it to them. They sank a Japanese battleship and received a Presidential citation for their work. Will Graves was given a medal for his bravery. Did your grandfather have the capacity to kill a man? You bet he did. But not murder. No sir."

"Wow, that's an incredible story," Anna said. It's hard for me to picture those big gentle hands doing anything like that at all." She wanted to know more.

# CHAPTER FOURTEEN

He told Anna how he had wanted to solve the biggest mystery the county ever had, but failed even after thirty-five years of trying. His main motivation had been to clear Will's name.

"I worked that case off and on for my entire career and never came close to solving it. Not one time. I don't think I'll ever know. I have read every scrap of paper and looked at every piece of evidence over and over and over. I know this case by heart. Newspaper articles, court filings, transcripts from the trial, everything."

"There was a trial," Anna asked, eyes wide.

"Will was arrested. There were several witnesses and a great deal of testimony at the probable cause hearing. The judge eventually threw it out based upon Mattie's testimony," Jack explained.

"Well, I think the evidence you are looking for is in the letters my grandmother left me and that have somehow disappeared."

"Listen, I'll run home and get my case file."

Upon his return Jack and Anna pieced the trial together by reading the transcript from the hearing and the newspaper articles.

*"Raise your right hand please."* Will Graves did as he was told.

*"Do you swear to tell the truth, the whole truth, and nothing but the truth, so help you God?"*

*"I do,"* Will said.

*"You may be seated."* Will Graves lowered his big right hand and sat down. It was the same hand he always extended whenever a neighbor needed one.

*"Please state your name,"* Homer Kent instructed his client.

*"Will Graves."*

*"Are you testifying today of your own free will and accord,"* the lawyer asked.

*"Yes."*

*"Have you been advised by me, your lawyer, that you do not have to testify?"*

*"Yes."*

*"Have you also been advised by me that you are testifying against my advice."* The lawyer was laying serious ground work to cover his rear end.

*"You told me not to testify,"* Will said.

*"Then why are you testifying?"*

*"Objection. Self serving, your Honor,"* the District Attorney interposed.

*"Overruled. We both know that all testimony is self serving. That's the point. I want to hear what the man has to say,"* Judge Brown ruled.

*"Go ahead and answer the question Mr. Graves,"* the Judge ordered.

*"Well, this whole thing is a bunch of bullshit,"* Will answered. *"I did not kill that man. Never liked him, but I did not kill him."*

*"We are not in the barn here. This is a courtroom and I expect that everyone here will treat it that way, including you Mr. Graves,"* Judge Brown admonished. *"Watch the language."*

*"Yes sir,"* Will said.

*"When was the last time you saw Sonny Howland alive,"* Kent asked.

*"The night of the fight. After he come to, the cops drug him off. I didn't see him after that."*

*"What started the fight?"*

*"Sonny insulted my wife,"* Will said.

*"Tell the Court what happened."*

*"When Mattie and I come in from dancing Howland said something to her when we walked by. So I hit him in the nose as hard as I could."*

*"What did he say to your wife, Will,"* Homer asked.

*"Don't know. Couldn't hear it."*

*"How do you know she was insulted if you didn't hear what he said?"*

*"I heard what she said to him. She called him a pig. That was enough for me."*

*"Did Mattie ever tell you what Sonny Howland said to her that evening?"*

*"No. She wouldn't do it. Said it was beneath her. So I let it rest."* As he said this, Will looked over at his wife who was seated in the first row directly behind counsel's table. Mattie sat with self-composed calmness. Stylish and beautiful, Mattie Graves sat in silent elegant support of her husband. He drew strength from her graceful courage.

*"Have you been in the courtroom throughout these entire proceedings?"*

*"Yes,"* he answered.

*"Have you heard the testimony about the fight from the others who have testified in this matter?"*

*"Yes I have,"* Will assured Homer.

*"Do you agree with their description of events?"*

*"Yes."*

*"Do you have anything to add?"*

*"Yes."*

*"Please continue,"* Homer prompted.

*"He was one tough son of a .... b."* There were a few snickers in the courtroom.

*"Enough of that. We will have order."* Judge Brown ended the moment with a tap of the gavel.

*"Continue Will,"* Judge Brown ordered.

*"I was fighting for my life that night. Howland wanted to kill me. I gave it everything I had. But if Mattie hadn't busted that beer bottle over his head I don't think I would be here to testify. Every one of you got the facts right. I just wanted you to know how it felt."*

*"Anything else?"*

*"I guess not,"* Will said.

*"Where were you on the night of August 21, 1950?"*

*"Home."*

*"All night?"*

*"Yes."*

*"Were you alone,"* Homer asked.

*"No. Mattie was home too."*

*"Anyone else at home with you on the night of the murder?"*

*"Just the dog."* This again drew a few chuckles from the gallery which the judge chose to ignore this time.

*"Describe what you did that day."*

*"When,"* Will asked. Homer instructed him to describe his entire day. Will went on to lay out a rather long hot summer day on the farm. From early morning to chores in the evening.

*"Anything else you can think of?"*

*"Well, I did take my usual afternoon nap."*

Ignoring Will's last response, Homer pressed on into Will's activities during the evening hours of that day.

*"This was a Saturday night wasn't it?"*

*"Sure was,"* Will answered.

*"You stayed home that entire evening?"*

*"Yes we did."*

*"Don't you and Mattie normally go out on Saturday night,"* Homer asked.

*"We usually do. But since the fight I haven't felt much like being around people,"* Will said.

*"Why is that?"*

*"I guess I am a little embarrassed."*

The judge ordered a short mid morning break. Will got down from the stand and came back to where Mattie stood waiting with a glass of water. He drank it down without stopping and returned the glass to her. She dabbed at his sweaty brow with her handkerchief, then gave him a squeeze of his hand and a peck on his cheek. By this time the judge was ready to go again.

*"All rise,"* the Bailiff called out. The courtroom rose in unison as the judge made his way back to the bench. The shock of pure white hair topped the smallish man in the black robe. He banged the gavel.

*"Be seated. Will, take the stand. You are already sworn. Counsel."* With that he turned it back over to Lawyer Kent. Homer moved a few papers around in front of him. When his own client was on the stand he liked to sit. He wanted the emphasis on his client.

*"Mr. Graves. Did you ever have any trouble with Sonny Howland before the night of the fight,"* Homer finally got around to asking after a lengthy pause. Homer used silence to get peoples attention.

*"Not once."*

*"Never,"* Homer wanted him to confirm the answer.

*"Never."*

*"What was your opinion of the man?"*

*"Not very good."*

*"Did you like him,"* Homer asked.

*"No, I did not."*

*"Did your family hold anything against him?"*

*"Our families never got along if that's what you mean,"* Will said.

*"Why is that?"*

*"It started back when our dads went to school together. Sonny's dad broke my old man's homemade skis. They were the fastest ones on the hill. Tug got his clock cleaned for that one. He run into the school house to hide behind the teacher's skirt, my dad followed him in and mopped up the floor with him,"* Will explained.

*"By Tug, you mean Sonny Howland's father,"* Kent asked.

"*Yeah. That's who I mean.*"

"*Did it end there, with that fight,*" Homer asked.

"*No sir. Back in the 30's Tug and some of the other neighbors joined the KKK and they tried to get us.*"

"*By the KKK do you mean the Ku Klux Klan,*" Homer asked.

"*That's it. Bunch of damn cowards is all they were. Went around scaring the daylights out of people. Burned crosses. Beat people up. Went around wearing hoods like we wouldn't know who they were. Damn fools.*"

"*Go on,*" Homer instructed.

"*They hated Catholics. There were not enough Negroes around to pick on I guess,*" Will said.

"*What did they do to you and your family?*"

"*They tried to beat up my dad and raid our house one night, but my dad scared 'em off.*"

"*Tell us about that please,*" Homer coached.

"*It started when Tug and a couple of his buddies stopped dad and I on the road one day when we were out grading. My old man just laughed at 'em. He grabbed that double bladed axe of his and chased them away. They fell all over themselves trying to get out of range of that axe. He kept it like a razor and everyone around knew it,*" Will said.

"*Anything else,*" Homer knew what was coming.

"*Besides burning a cross in the field across the road, they stopped at our house. Two cars stopped out by the mail box with their lights off. My dad was in the front door and I was upstairs. We both had loaded shotguns. Dad hollered out up to me to shoot the first s.o.b. that stepped out of the car. I guess they thought he meant it. They drove off.*" It seemed clear to everyone that Will enjoyed telling this part of the story.

"*Did Tug Howland eventually stop bothering his neighbors,*" Homer asked.

"*He sure did.*"

"*How did it end?*"

"*One night my dad and a few other neighbors snuck up on the Klan's meeting place out by Dismal Creek. My dad came up behind Tug Howland*

*and put a cocked 12 gauge shotgun up against the back of his head. He told him that 'it ends right here, right now.' Either they stopped, or Tug was going to be separated from this life. That ended it."*

*"Is Dismal Creek where they found the body of Sonny Howland?"*

*"Same place,"* Will confirmed. Homer knew that this piece of information was not helpful to the case. However, there was no sense waiting for the District Attorney to drag it out and make it look like it was part of his case. Homer much preferred to bring bad points out when he did the questioning. It somehow lessened the sting.

*"And you believe that these incidents are at the heart of the bad feelings between the Graves and Howland families,"* Homer asked.

*"Yes I do."*

Homer wasn't much to look at as a lawyer goes. A little frumpy, often a little too folksy, and maybe a bit distracted. He was often described as unorganized. It was all show. Homer Kent had one of the keenest legal minds around and he used his country lawyer persona to secure victory after victory throughout a very long career. He liked to slip in questions that were designed to surprise the person testifying. He even did this to his clients. He wanted critical questions to be answered spontaneously and without rehearsal. Homer stood up for emphasis.

*"Will, did you kill Sonny Howland,"* he asked point blank.

*"No I did not, damn it. How many times do I have to say it before anyone will believe me,"* came the emphatic unrehearsed reply.

*"That's all I have for now your Honor,"* and with that, Homer sat down. This was something else he had learned early on in the practice of law. If you score a point, shut up and sit down.

The District Attorney ripped into Will the best he could. He tried to paint the picture as one of bitter revenge. Will would have none of it and went toe to toe with the prosecutor for over an hour. Homer was very satisfied with his client's performance and declined to exercise his rebuttal. Will had told it all and further exploration would only aggravate the judge.

The gavel rapped twice and everyone left for lunch with the judge instructing the participants to *"be back by 1:30."*

Homer took the time to go over Mattie's testimony. She was to be next on the stand. Court resumed at the appropriate hour and after preliminaries Homer Kent asked Mattie Graves, *"Where were you on the night of August 21, 1950?"*

*"At home."*

*"Is there anything special or unique about that night which would cause you to remember it?"* Homer framed the question as an assertion which drew a D.A. objection.

*"Sustained. Leading,"* the judge ruled.

*"What were you doing that night,"* Homer asked reframing the question.

*"It was close to school opening and I was getting ready."*

*"You are a school teacher, correct?"*

*"Yes I am,"* Mattie answered.

*"Can you tell the Court how you know it was the night of August 21 that you were getting ready for school?"* Homer loved it when he knew he had evidence so solid it would lend credibility to everything else a witness said on the stand.

*"Because I date all of my work,"* she said.

Homer was up and moving to the Clerk's table with a small packet of papers. As the Clerk affixed the packet with an exhibit sticker, Homer rocked expectantly on the balls of his feet.

*"Mrs. Graves I show you Exhibit 1. Can you tell the Court what it is,"* Homer asked.

*"These are the papers I was working on,"* Mattie answered.

*"Did you date them?"*

*"Yes I did."*

*"And what is the date on the papers?"*

*"August 21, 1950,"* Mattie said.

After a pause that was long enough to be noticeable and to focus everyone's attention, Homer motioned towards the back of the courtroom for someone to come forward. Hank Delaney wheeled in three medium size boxes on a small handcart to the front of the courtroom. After Hank removed the dolly and returned to the back of the courtroom, Homer resumed his march towards the truth.

*"What are in these boxes Mrs. Graves?"*

*"All of my lesson plans for all of the years I have taught school?"*

*"Are they all dated?"*

*"Every single one,"* Mattie assured the Court. At that, Attorney Kent sank with slow satisfaction into his wooden counsel's chair. Mattie's demeanor was one of quiet confidence and grace. Homer resumed.

*"On August 21, 1950 what specifically were you working on?"*

*"An introduction to poetry using the work of Robert Frost. It is how I start every year."*

*"How long did it take you to prepare your lesson plan,"* he asked.

*"Hours. It is always my first lesson plan of the year and my favorite subject. I like to start my year in delight,"* she related with genuine warmth.

*"What time of the day did you work on your plan?"*

*"Late evening,"* she recalled.

*"Where was your husband while you were preparing your lesson plan on Robert Frost?"*

*"At home. In bed for much of the time."*

With a few clean up questions Homer nailed down the fact that at the time of the murder, Will Graves was at home with his wife, asleep. He closed his case by informing Judge Brown that he had, *"no further questions of Mrs. Graves and no further witnesses, your Honor."*

The D.A. was no slouch himself when it came to courtroom skills. He knew that if he could find out why a gentle man hit a rabid dog, he'd win the case. So he hammered away on the fight in the bar. In excruciating detail, he led Mattie through the night of the fight.

*"Mrs. Graves, your husband testified that Sonny Howland made a provocative comment to you as you left the dance floor. Do you recall that testimony,"* the D. A. asked.

*"Yes I do,"* she answered softly.

*"You agree that Sonny Howland made a comment to you that was offensive."*

*"Yes, I agree."*

*"What did he say to you?"*

*Mattie sat perfectly still looking at the prosecutor with her hands folded in her lap.*

*"Mrs. Graves I need an answer,"* he prompted. Mattie lifted her chin slightly and took in a short breath.

*"I am sorry but I will not repeat such a vile statement."*

*"I understand how difficult this may be for you, but you are required to answer this question. What did he say to you,"* he asked with some force. Mattie remained quiet now looking down at her hands.

*"Your Honor, would you please instruct the witness to answer,"* the D.A. requested the Court's help.

*"Mrs. Graves please give us your answer. If you refuse you could be found in contempt of court,"* Judge Brown said.

Mattie looked up at the Judge and held his gaze momentarily before looking back at the D.A. She let out a breath then composed herself for her answer.

*"I do not mean any disrespect, but if I repeated what that, that man said, I would be holding myself in contempt. Some things do not deserve repetition and this is one of them. You can do to me whatever you wish, but I am not going to repeat such garbage. Case closed."*

The D.A. pleaded and threatened. He rephrased and repeated. He asked the Court's help and he demanded justice. He stood, then he sat. He bellowed then he whispered. In short, the D.A. tried everything he could think of doing before finally asking the Court to find her in contempt of court for failing to answer and to lock her up until she answered the question. The Judge scratched his head, took his glasses off, then rubbed his eyes as if that would make the problem go away.

The Judge was also aware that the most prominent man in the county was sitting quietly in the back of the courtroom. It appeared to all present that Henry Beret was there to support his daughter, but it was noted that they did not speak.

Putting his glasses back on, Judge Brown leaned forward on the bench and looked at Mattie Graves who sat in dignified defiance. The Judge leaned on his elbows with his hands clasped in front of him then looked at the D.A., "*What would you have me do here? She is not going to answer the question if I put her into jail for a hundred years. It appears that no amount of pleading or threats is going to change that. Alright, I find you in contempt of court and fine you $50.00. Next question.*" And that was it. No one except Mattie would ever know the content of the slur.

The D.A. argued that there were just too many coincidences, too much circumstantial evidence, and too many connections between these people for the Judge to dismiss this case. He argued that it must go forward to trial. He further argued that there was more than enough probable cause to bind Will Graves over to be tried by the people of Brunswick County. Although Will's alibi might be tight, it had to be discounted because his wife would obviously back him up. It was not the D.A.'s day. Judge Brown had made up his mind.

Based on all the testimony, most especially Mattie's, the Judge found that Will Graves' alibi was solid and credible. With a bang of the gavel, the matter was dismissed and Will Graves walked out of the courtroom a free man holding his wife's hand. Although officially he was exonerated, most everyone thought he had to be the one.

Not a word had been said by the Assistant District Attorney who had been present throughout the entire proceeding. Assistant D.A. Thomas Fitzgerald sat in stone faced silence as the witnesses came and went throughout the preliminary hearing. From time to time he would pass a note to the D.A. Generally he avoided all eye contact. Rebecca Moore Fitzgerald also attended the preliminary hearing in support of her best friend Mattie and her husband even though they represented two sides of a fence for everyone knew that she and Mattie were best of friends.

By the time Jack finished the story the sun was up. Both Jack and Anna were blurry eyed and exhausted. Anna went upstairs to bed and Jack took Harry and went home. They promised to be in touch with each other soon. It had been a long night.

# CHAPTER FIFTEEN

Jack needed to go on patrol. He needed to clear his head and a ride would do him good. So he loaded his old dog into his old truck and headed out on an old quest. To find the truth. That's what it had always been about for Jack. A simple search for the truth or at least an understanding of the truth. Certainty was not always required. After all, he speculated, Einstein's was a theory of relativity, not certainty. But truth nonetheless.

To find that truth he drove to the cemetery on the bluff above the Graves farm. It had been plowed so Jack drove to the back of the cemetery and got out of the truck, leaving Harry inside. He walked through the snow to the edge of the bluff and looked down at the farm house which was darkened except for the light in the pantry. Jack pictured Anna writing at her desk.

The previous evening at the farm had been quite the experience. It was not often that he had the individual attention of a pretty woman for so many hours. She had given him a peck on the cheek when he left. He could still feel the brush of her lips. Her breath had the sweet smell of wine and coffee. So what was the truth in how he was feeling about all that, he wondered.

Jack watched a car round the corner at the top of the hill and descend into the valley. The car passed from his right to his left past the Graves farm below and on down the valley. He thought that anyone could keep pretty close track of things on the Graves farm from this spot. More than once lately he had a funny feeling when passing this way. Inexplicably he would feel a chill. He did not know what to attribute the feeling to, although his cop's instinct told him not to discount it. But right now his cop's instinct, usually sharp, was blurred by the bright light of a woman.

Jack returned to the truck and opened his thermos of coffee. Harry came over and put his cold nose in Jack's ear then gave him a lick. Rubbing the dog's big head he gave him a "hey buddy." They sat with the lights off and the truck idling. Cold winter air came in through the open windows and cooled the interior of the cab so he turned up the fan a notch and felt heat rise up from under the dash. Jack was content to remain part of the night, sitting still, thinking.

Many years before Jack had sat in this very same spot in the embrace of Cindy Robertson. She was the only other woman who ever warmed his heart. They often used the cemetery as their last stop on the way home after a date. That particular night after some very tender loving moments, Cindy told Jack about the baby. Jack was eighteen and Cindy was sixteen. Shocked as he was, Jack clearly and firmly decided that marriage would follow. Cindy, so totally relieved by his love and support, cried in his arms for a long time.

Jack turned on the lights of the truck and slowly followed the same route out of the cemetery over Cemetery Road to the stop sign. There, just as he had that evening so many years before, he turned left onto Stoney Lonesome Road. Going only a short distance he came to the point where the road tops out on the ridge and begins to curve down into the valley. He stopped here just as he and Cindy had done that night. He had shut the lights off in order to admire the moon lit valley below. It was a night much like the one Jack was experiencing.

He would never forget the impact of Doyle Howland's car slamming into them from behind. It drove them over the bank where they rolled and came to rest against a big oak tree. Although Doyle was drunk and driving way too fast, the accident was definitely Jack's fault. Losing the baby left deep cuts to her heart and scars on their relationship that could not be repaired. For more than thirty-five years, their relationship remained in the limbo it was thrown into on the night of the accident.

She was the only other girl he ever loved, but the forces that kept them apart were too large for Jack to understand. Sometimes the whole thing left him confused, even angry. It was as if they were locked in this weird dance where they never fully committed, nor did they ever fully let go. He often thought that they had the same relationship as the Big and Little Dipper. They were locked in a timeless embrace, circling around a faint star, just like the faded love between them.

Jack turned his headlights on and eased out the clutch beginning his descent into the valley. He drove slowly past the farm which was still lit by the soft glow of the pantry light. Once past the farm, Jack and Harry crossed the narrow bridge and turned up the steep incline that went past the Howland place. Tonight Doyle's Caddy had the company of a rusted out white Ford. Doyle and Sally were at it again. Sally was a sometime squeeze of Doyle's from the north side bar scene. They fought as often as they fornicated.

Doyle's trailer house was dark. It was near 3 a.m. and tonight Howland had followed his usual pattern. But Doyle's nightly routine had changed over the last few months. He was not in his normal places at the normal times and that bothered Jack. He didn't know what to make of it, but Jack would be watching. Provided that he could clear his head long enough to get a clear view.

Driving along he wondered again about the missing letters Anna told him about. They could be the key to unlocking the entire Howland murder mystery. Even more puzzling was who would have known about them and why were they taken. He did not believe for one minute that they were misplaced accidentally or destroyed at the last minute by Mattie. Someone got into that house and took them. It had to be someone with prior knowledge of the letters and the murder. Although he was now aware of additional evidence which could possibly crack the case, it did him no good. He was right back where he had always been. Another dead end. He was no closer to the truth of the case or of his life than he had been before his nightly patrol.

# CHAPTER SIXTEEN

Anna had gone to bed after Jack left the house and she stayed there all day until well after dark. It had been a very long time since she stayed up all night. Topping the lack of sleep off with copious amounts of alcohol and THC kept her head under the pillow for nearly twelve hours. It had been worth the effort.

She followed her 3 a.m. coffee ritual and drove to the Brunswick Café to contemplate. Bud and Theresa had run the café and adjoining bakery for more than 30 years. When Theresa died a few years back, Bud decided to open the café at night.

Anna had become a regular. From her favorite corner booth she observed the comings and goings of café patrons and activities outside. She was settled in with a mug of steaming coffee when she noticed the faded blue pickup truck pass by her window. Anna smiled at the thought of Harry in his place next to the retired cop in the cab of that comfortable old truck.

Her middle of the night visits to a coffee shop began while in Madison. Preferring to study late at night when there were few distractions, she got into the habit of taking a late coffee break.

"Refill?" Anna looked away from the window to see an apron clad Bud holding a pot of fresh coffee in anticipation of topping off her mug.

"Thanks."

"I sure appreciate the business and the company," Bud said through his smile.

"I love coming in here," Anna assured the old man. "Besides, where else am I going to get a great cup of coffee this time of night," she added.

"You got that right. The sign says it all," he nodded and pointed at the sign above the grill. They shared a laugh while reading the sign out loud together "Best Damn Coffee in the World."

Growing serious, Bud told Anna that from now on this booth would be "the poet's corner," reserved just for her. He had noticed the poetry book she always brought along. "That's awfully nice Bud, thank you," Anna replied.

"Any time young lady." With that, Bud returned to his baking duties and Anna returned to her favorite Frost Reader.

Anna liked to read poetry of all kinds, but she never failed to reread a few favorites from Robert Frost. His rhythms, rhymes, and insights into human nature were fused with the cadence of her own life. Most children grow up with the "cow jumped over the moon." Anna grew up with "Nothing Gold Can Stay."

Between her scholarly father and literary minded grandmother, Anna's poetic heritage was sound. She rarely confronted a problem without first dusting off the words of her favorite bard. As usual, whenever a choice loomed, Anna turned to Frost's "The Road Not Taken." For her the poem represented the fork in the road and the consequences of taking one path over the other. In teaching Anna this poem, Mattie had gently instructed, "Remember, your life will be dictated by the choices you make." According to Grams, consequences were the by-products of free will.

Anna thought about Jack Delaney. A relationship was brewing. The smile on her heart had grown since Harry and Jack had shown up at her front door to fix the roof. It widened every time she was in his presence. Now he had asked her to a dance. Almost as an afterthought to the long night of familial revelation, Jack had mentioned the upcoming Saturday night dance at Hank's Place. Without thinking she had said "I'd love to go," and so it was a date.

Anna read through a few poems then turned to the inside cover of the book. There in the beautiful flowing handwriting of her grandmother, she read, "To Anna, read this book and read it again. Carry it with you throughout your life. There is more wisdom in these words than I will ever be able to teach you. As you experience life they will change in meaning as you grow. Enjoy. Love, Grams."

She had been given the Frost Reader on her sixteenth birthday. It had been her constant companion for twenty years. Anna finished her coffee, waved goodnight to Bud, then drove home to the little farm on Stoney Lonesome Road by the light of the full moon.

# CHAPTER SEVENTEEN

The parking lot at Hank's Place was full by the time they arrived. What started out as a lark to have a couple of the boys play a little music had turned into a full fledged dance by Saturday night. It had been a long time since anyone had danced to live music on this corner.

Turned faces, smiles, smoke, hellos, handshakes, laughter, and the noise of a packed bar greeted them as they walked in the back door. Everyone knew Jack. No one knew Anna. He introduced her as best he could as they made their way through the crowd to the bar for a drink. By the time they finally made it, both of them needed one.

"What are you going to have, good looking," Cindy asked as she greeted Jack in her usual way while at the same time eye-balling the very pretty and much younger woman who was with him.

"Hi Cindy, um, what would you like," he asked Anna.

"A beer would be fine. Any kind is okay."

"Couple of Leinie's will do," he said as he ordered and paid. Cindy moved away after serving them and before Jack had the chance to introduce Anna.

"That's Cindy. We grew up together," Jack said.

They clicked bottle necks and each took a swig in celebration of the evening about to begin. Herb was on the raised platform in the corner that functioned as a stage. Herb looked pretty good tuning up his old guitar. He had his best western shirt on and had honored the evening with a string tie. His black pants were pressed, his thin hair slicked straight back, and his cowboy boots where shined. Jack thought he was the boniest man he had ever seen in his life. Backing up Herb was a gray haired keyboard player and a Jimmy Buffet look alike on guitar.

Hank's Place was once again filled with the people of Brunswick. Although a few old timers were present for the reunion, most were keeping each other company up on cemetery ridge. Jack's generation had taken its place next in line. He mixed with neighbors and friends from a life time. Sprinkled throughout the crowd were old girl friends, school mates, and kids he had ridden the bus with a million years ago.

Herb and company let her rip. No one had heard Herb wail like that in quite a while. It wasn't long before the dance floor was full, feet were tapping, and folks were singing along. Herb was once again the master of his kingdom with the crowd at his feet.

The crowd roared for more. After a few sets of good old time rock and roll, Herb and the boys switched to a set of two steps, followed by polkas. When they settled into a waltz, Jack asked Anna to dance. She declined, not knowing how to waltz. A further offer to teach her the fine points was met with a "not yet." Anna was not about to make her Brunswick debut by stepping on Jack's feet.

"Cindy, go dance with Jack," someone at the bar suggested.

"Yeah, you guys should have a dance," another agreed.

"Well good lookin', what do you think, should we," Cindy challenged him across the bar.

"Absolutely," Jack accepted. Around they went. One, two, three. One, two, three.

They danced as one might expect a couple who had done so for four decades. As Anna watched them dance, she was surprised at the jealousy that rose within her. They looked good together. After the dance, Jack and Anna made their way to the elbow in the bar which was occupied by the brandy drinking Father Daniel. "Evening Reverend," Jack said as they warmly shook hands.

"You know Anna McCucheon," he said as he presented her to the good Father.

"Hello Father."

"Of course, of course. Nice to see you again Ms. McCucheon. Let's have a drink. What'll you have my dear," he asked. Anna held up her empty bottle of Leinie's.

"Cindy," Father Dan shouted over the din and made the universal circular motion of ordering a round. Cindy acknowledged with a raised index finger and a nod indicating the drinks would be right up in a moment.

"Saving souls tonight Father," Jack teased the clearly inebriated priest.

"Laddy, if they are anything like me, they haven't got a chance. Pious on the outside. Porous on the inside," he laughed heartily at his own joke. When the cleric was in his cups he often lapsed into a faux Irish brogue.

"Danny boy, you had better take it easy or I'll have to drive you home," Cindy admonished him irreverently as she served up the round and collected the payment from a small pile of cash on the bar.

"Now Sis, don't you be mother'n the father. Your big brother will be taken care of hisself."

"Yeah, right. Give me those keys," she ordered and held out her hand. "Come on, hand 'em over." Father Dan slowly reached into his pocket for his keys and delicately dropped them into her open hand. "There you go Lass, now will you please let me drink with reckless abandon," he asked.

"Be my guest." She said tossing the keys into a basket on the back bar, then went about serving other customers bearing a satisfied look on her face.

Jack explained to Anna that Father Dan and Cindy were brother and sister. Father Dan further elaborated on his family structure, "Don't you be forgettin' our big brother Herb the headliner over there." They all turned to see Herb strumming and singing away. "The last of the Robertsons we are. Not a one of us has any children. Herb's the oldest, Cindy is the baby, and I'm stuck in the middle," he explained. With that, the good Father launched into one of his raunchy dirty jokes told in his best Irish brogue to anyone who would listen.

One unfortunate feature of the Saturday night dance at Hank's had always been the presence of a Howland. Tonight was no exception. Doyle was getting drunker and louder by the beer. Being obnoxious would have been an improvement. Jack had kept a wary eye on him since he walked in the front door and rudely made his way to the bar demanding immediate attention.

Everyone gave Doyle a wide berth. At the moment he was trying to pick a fight with Father Dan who was doing his priestly best to ignore him. Jack stood close enough to hear and act if necessary.

"You never liked my family did you," Doyle accused.

"Doyle lad, I have been through this with you time and again. I hold nothing ill in me heart for any of God's creatures," he said, refusing to rise to the bait. Jack could see that Doyle was in his usual foul mood. He then turned his verbal guns on a woman seated next to him at the bar.

As Doyle headed for the bathroom he said loudly "I gotta piss," and stumbled through the crowd. Jack followed him into the bathroom after posting a guard at the door. Doyle leaned his forehead up against the mirror on the wall above the urinal doing his business. Jack pulled a snub-nosed .38 caliber revolver from his coat pocket, walked up to Doyle, and stuck it in his ear. Howland stiffened but did not move away.

"Now listen to me, you piece of shit. I'm only going to say this once. You ruin this night for Cindy and I'm going to ruin you. Understand?"

"You talk pretty fuckin' big with a gun in your hand, don't ya," Doyle responded as he looked ahead at the reflections in the mirror.

"It's the only God damn thing you pig headed fucking Howlands seem to understand." It had been Jack's experience that only the threat of a gun got Doyle's attention. "Now, you get your sorry ass out of this bar," Jack ordered Doyle. He slipped the gun back in his pocket and left the room.

After Jack walked out, Doyle thought, alright cop, you win this one. He could have cared less if Delaney pulled the trigger. In fact he would be doing him a favor if he did so. But he had unfinished business to attend to and nothing was going to stop him. He'd take the cop out too if he got in his way. Everyone noticed that Doyle left the bar quietly when he exited the bathroom.

As Jack returned to his place next to Anna and Father Dan, Cindy caught his eye and silently mouthed, "thank you" from behind the bar. He nodded and returned to his beer.

"What was that all about," Anna asked. Father Dan chuckled beside them and said "it appears that Jack here pointed out the facts of life to Mister Howland."

"Reckon so," Jack confirmed. The night progressed drunkenly towards its end without further incident. Jack and Anna danced to a few rock numbers. Herb and the boys ended the evening howling at a blue moon.

They made their way down Stoney Lonesome Road towards the farm. As they neared Cemetery Road he asked if he could show her something. Affirmed, he turned towards the cemetery. From the back of the cemetery, Jack showed Anna the little farm below.

The valley spread out away from them in the quiet moon filled night. "Can you find the North Star," he asked after standing quietly together for a few moments.

"Isn't it that bright one right there," she pointed at a bright star in the north.

"Most people think the North Star is the brightest in the sky, but they are wrong. It's right there. See that faint one." He directed her line of sight along the line of his extended arm and finger.

"I see it," Anna said.

"That's the North Star. It's the first star in the handle of the Little Dipper. Follow the arc. That's the handle. Right there. The Little Dipper is always opposite the Big Dipper. They circle each other in the night sky. It's a dance that has gone on for billions and billions of years. So now you can always find the North Star," he said. Anna turned and kissed Jack Delaney with her heart on her lips.

# CHAPTER EIGHTEEN

Somewhere in the deep recesses of his unconscious state Jack heard the ringing phone. He came to sleepy awareness when Anna answered its call.

"Hello. Yes this is. Yes he is. Just a moment." She covered the receiver and told him the hospital was on the line. Jack sat up in the bed and took the phone shaking off the last vestige of deep sleep.

"Jack Delaney."

"Mr. Delaney. I am so sorry to bother you this early, but Mrs. Fitzgerald insisted we call you. She has been asking for you," the nurse explained. Jack had given Anna's phone number to the hospital as a way to reach him if needed.

"Is she alright," he asked.

"Stable, but very weak. She has become increasingly anxious and she will not take no for an answer. I am really sorry about this intrusion," she apologized. It was 6:00 a.m.

"No, no, that's alright. Not a problem. Tell her I'll be right there." Jack handed the phone back to Anna and filled her in as he began getting dressed. "I have to go."

"I'm coming with you," Anna said as she jumped out of bed and threw on some clothes. Following the dance, Jack and Anna had been virtually inseparable for days. Late nights, long talks, and copious copulation had filled their time. In truth, Jack had been neglecting the widow.

They found the widow's bone thin body curled beneath the covers in a fetal position. Jack barely recognized her gray features. He wasn't even sure if she was alive until her eyes fluttered open. She was already in the middle distance between this life and the next. Jack had seen enough death to know when it presented itself to collect yet another payment. He was shocked at how much she had deteriorated in just the last few days.

"Mrs. Fitzgerald, it's Jack," he said as he touched her shoulder and leaned in close. He was not sure she had heard him until the faded eyes turned his way and a faint smile appeared.

"Thank God you are here," she said in the weakest of voices. Clearly, life's energy had run the course. He knew with certainty that it was just a matter of time.

"I must see Thomas."

"Pardon me," he was not sure he had heard her correctly.

"Thomas. I must see his face one more time," she paused as if marshaling all of her strength just to talk. Jack waited with patience. After a few moments she continued.

"By my bed...at home...his picture...my favorite...please...I must see it," she managed.

"I'll go get it right away," he promised. Death's hand made another pass at Rebecca Moore Fitzgerald and she lapsed back into deep sleep, spent.

"I'll stay," Anna volunteered as Jack left to get the picture. Anna quietly sat in the chair by the bed, watching the dying woman sleep.

He returned with a beautifully framed black and white photo of Thomas Fitzgerald. The widow was sleeping peacefully so Jack placed it next to the bed. It would be the first thing she noticed when she opened her eyes. Assuming she would do so again.

While Jack checked on Mrs. Fitzgerald's condition at the nurses station, Anna sat next to the bed studying the picture of Mr. Fitzgerald. He stood on the front steps of the law school smoking a cigarette. He was clad in a suit and had a smirk on his face, the image drawing her in. Although she didn't know why, it seemed familiar even though she had never seen Thomas Fitzgerald in her life.

They made sure the staff had all the necessary contact information before leaving. Jack and Anna stopped at the Brunswick Café for coffee and an early breakfast. The "poet's corner" was open so they slid into the booth.

"So this is where you spend your late nights," Jack stated after the waitress had taken their order and left.

"This is it. Bud told me the other night that this is now 'my' spot," Anna said as she made the quotation mark gesture around the "my" for emphasis. She went on to explain to Jack the background for her late night coffee habit.

Changing the subject, they talked at length about the widow. Anna wanted to know how Mr. Fitzgerald had died and when.

"He was killed in an accidental shooting. He was a big hunter and gun collector. His huge gun collection is still in that big old house. Anyway, he accidentally shot himself while he was cleaning a rifle," Jack explained.

"At home?"

"Yeah, in the basement where he kept his guns. The widow found him. Actually heard the shot I guess. Never got over it."

"I'm not so sure I should stay around here. It seems pretty dangerous. Maybe I should move back to Phoenix where it's safe," Anna half joked. They talked about the old Fitzgerald house and the widow's plan for it all.

"You mean she has been living alone since 1963. Never remarried?"

"Not even a boyfriend as far as I know," Jack said.

"I can't believe that she is just going to give it all away and leave you high and dry after taking care of her all these years."

"Well, she lived for her husband. He was her life and her focus. It's alright. The more stuff you own, the more it owns you anyway," he philosophized with a shrug of his shoulders. Jack's need for money had always been a low priority.

About the time their cups needed refilling, Jack noticed Cindy walking in the front door. She proceeded to the counter and from her gestures it was clear a takeout bakery order was in progress. As her order was being processed, Cindy glanced around the room. Her glance froze on the corner booth and Jack. She nodded. He waved. Anna turned to look. Cindy paid her bill and left with a white bag of goodies.

"Can I ask you a question," she asked with trepidation, knocking on a door behind which she didn't know what lay.

"Sure," Jack knew where this was going. It was that period in a new relationship when you began to discover each other's baggage.

"Its kinda personal," she gave him one more chance to tell her to mind her own business.

"If it gets too hot I'll let you know," he assured her.

"I get the impression that you and Cindy are more than old schoolmates."

"We dated some in high school. We have been friends since," acknowledging her point without disclosing any detail. Anna simply said, "Oh," and went back to her coffee. The tension was broken with the arrival of their food. Over breakfast the discussion turned back to the Howland murder. Jack wondered aloud about the letters' connection to the case.

"Someone wrote to your grandmother about the murder it seems. Probably a friend who was directly connected or knew someone involved," Jack said.

"But why would Grams refuse to talk about it?"

"I suppose she was trying to protect someone," he said.

"But who was she trying to protect?"

"If we knew that we'd be a lot closer to solving this thing. And what was the reference to a painful period in her life all about? Was she somehow involved? Is that even possible?" Shaking his head Jack took a sip of hot coffee holding the cup in both hands with his elbows on the table. "It makes my head hurt just to think about all of it."

It had been snowing for awhile by the time Jack and Anna checked on the mansion and picked up the mail. Anna had not been to either Mrs. Fitzgerald's place or Jack's small house. She was amazed by the size and warmth differences in the two places. Although it was beautiful, the mansion was spatially large and esthetically cold. Jack's carriage house was small and filled with warmth by comparison.

"What have you got for supplies at your house," Jack asked. "This is going to last for quite a while and my bet is we are going to be snowed in," he explained. It was one hell of a snowstorm. Under the same circumstances, they did what any self-respecting Wisconsinite would do, stocking up on pizza, movies, and beer. They shared a batten-down-the-hatches moment plowing through the thick snow covered road. It snowed and blew for two days. On the morning the sky cleared Anna was awakened by Harry licking her face. Harry had settled into the farm house as if it were home.

"Hi Harry," she sleepily greeted the dog who persisted licking her entire face. She hugged him and giggled which caused a stir next to her.

"I think you want to go out, don't you boy," Anna said to Harry, who, upon hearing the words "go out" bounded to the door. Anna shuffled to the kitchen and let Harry out through the porch. She thought that he was the lickingest dog she had ever met in her life.

She went about firing the stove and making coffee while surveying the kitchen and pantry. Anna had found the boxes of work from Mattie's teaching life along with her journals. These items were arrayed on the kitchen table and floor along with Jack's file on the murder. Jack had repeatedly called the hospital to check on the widow whose condition remained unchanged.

They had been systematically going through everything to see if anything at all shed light on the current events regarding the missing letters. They continued to focus on Will Graves' trial. Anna found a short poem penned by Mattie the day of her testimony. She once again read the poem while enjoying her morning coffee. Early morning light from the rising sun shown onto Will's rocker. It was so inviting that Anna moved from the table to the chair with her grandmother's journal and her grandad's coffee cup.

Anna was unsure of the poem's meaning or whether it was of any real significance other than as an outlet for the anxiety her grandmother must have been feeling about the entire episode. She read,

## Today

Today I do nothing more
than I must,
nothing more,
nothing less,
just.

She was impressed with Jack's ability to analyze the bits and scraps of evidence, like this poem, in a meticulous yet open minded way. He did not jump to conclusions, merely letting the evidence speak for itself.

While Anna had been at Jack's house retrieving the mail, she had read the framed citation hanging on his living room wall. It was given to him for thirty-five years of service to the Sheriff's Department on the day of his retirement. The citation said that Jack had been selected as the Department's "Officer of the Year." It also read that while he was a detective, he had "solved" every major case he had been assigned. She noted with a certain poignancy that below that last sentence Jack had penned in his own hand "except one." She knew that the editorial comment referred to the unsolved Howland murder. Before long, Jack was awake sharing coffee and speculation with Anna.

"Up to now, there has been one motive for the murder and that was the family feud," he explained.

"But now we know that someone else had knowledge of the murder or some other involvement in it. That information provides us with a different motive and could unlock this case," Jack ruminated as he sipped coffee and stared at the floor lost in thought. Anna sat quietly in the rocker, listening.

"The point is," he said as he looked up at Anna "the letters present a second motive not present up until now. But the who and why are big questions still unanswered," Jack said while scratching his head. "We have to find those letters."

"Maybe we should take a break. Let's think about something else for a while," she smiled.

"Do you have anything in mind," he asked returning the smile. She took his coffee cup away from him and placed it on the table. Taking him by the hand, Anna led Jack up the stairs.

# CHAPTER NINETEEN

I t always gave Cindy pause to see Jack Delaney with another woman. She accepted that she had no rights to him, but always felt that Jack was her guy.

Cindy finished washing the glasses and began wiping down the bar. She worked hard to keep the place clean even when she didn't expect much business, like today. The snowstorm had all but shut down any travel. Only the most hardy or foolish ventured out.

As she worked, Cindy thought further about Jack Delaney. They had been high school sweethearts. He was a senior when she was a sophomore. They basically grew up together. When she turned sixteen, his eighteen year old libido shifted into high gear. She began to notice the general attention from boys she was getting wearing her cashmere sweater. Jack was no exception. For her, he had always been the one. Her heart had never belonged to anyone else since the day they started dancing together at a young age.

Cindy wore his ring for a year and a half. The first time they made love was indelibly inked in her mind. She could still feel the warm breeze as they lay on a blanket behind the old windmill on a hill behind her house. Afterwards, they lay side by side looking up at the sky. The moonlight reflected softly off their naked bodies. Jack showed her how to find the North Star. Whenever she looked up at the sky, Cindy thought about that night. She could still see him drawing a map across the sky for her to find it.

She didn't mean to get pregnant. It just happened. They thought they had things covered in that department, but the timing was a little off. So Jack's response to the news cemented her love for him forever. Without skipping a beat he said that they would get married. She had been so scared to tell him about the baby, but he reacted with support and love. They made love at the back of the cemetery on the bluff overlooking the Graves farm. On the way home they stopped at the top of the hill to look at the moon.

It was the last thing she remembered until waking up in the hospital. They told her she had retrograde amnesia. Her memory was wiped clean from that last tender moment until she awoke at the hospital. Cindy had no recollection of the accident. It turned out that the baby's loss was the only chance she would ever have to give birth. The injuries she suffered left her unable to conceive.

Cindy stared out the front window as the wind and snow swirled and blew. She supposed it was kind of funny, but she had bought the bar in part to hang onto something they had had together. When Hank's arthritis and age hampered his ability to run the bar, Cindy started helping out part time. It grew into a full-time job and spilled over into caring for Jack's father. His condition rendered him house bound.

Eventually, Cindy moved into the apartment above the bar, completely took over running the business, and became Hank's full-time care giver. Jack came around as needed. Although he helped in caring for his father, Cindy carried most of the water in that regard. Her actions had brought her closer to Jack than at any time since the accident. His middle of the night visits had increased for a time.

Over the years Jack and Cindy had seen each other on occasion. Sometimes at her instigation and sometimes at his. Both were involved with others, but they kept a place in their hearts for each other. This new woman felt different, however. Jack looked at Anna differently. It was the way he used to look at her back in high school. For some reason, probably old fashioned woman's intuition, she sensed a change. Cindy realized she was crying, tears wetting her cheeks.

The snowplow went by the bar in a cloud of snow. For the first time, in a long time, Cindy closed Hank's Place. Shutting off the lights and locking the door, she went upstairs to her apartment and curled up on her couch clutching her pain and fear to her chest.

# CHAPTER TWENTY

Harry was in his place with his head out the passenger window. The soft spring air flowing through the cab felt good. Anna snuggled next to Jack as he drove. With the patrol over they turned into the driveway. Anna accepted Jack's need to drift and watch while not understanding it entirely. She was grateful he brought her with on occasion.

"I'll be along in a minute," Jack informed Anna upon parking the truck. Harry ran off in the dark and she went into the house. From his vantage point he surveyed the house and yard. He watched as Harry sniffed around the machine shed.

The spring wind made him think of Mrs. Fitzgerald. It had always been the widow's favorite time of the year. Her death had been unsettling and the feeling generated by her loss was something akin to losing a parent. A mother figure to be more accurate.

Leaning against the fender of his pickup, Jack gazed at the partial moon and the stars through the colorless trees. Hold over oak leaves sang their last chorus. Already, new buds were breaking out and would force the last of the leaves onto the ground.

Jack crawled up on the hood of his truck and lay back against the windshield. Looking up towards the southwest he located the Subaru Sisters. When he looked directly at the cluster of stars, they faded. When he shifted his focus just to the side of the same faded group of stars, they came into focus. He thought that his life was as distorted as Subaru. The harder he looked at it, the fuzzier it appeared. Staring up at the heavens, he thought of his mother. It was she who had taught him about the stars.

He possessed no memory of his mother living at home above the tavern. According to the stories he had heard at the bar, Dorothy Delaney left Hank for another man. At first Jack had gone with his mother. Within a short time however, her new man, who was unsympathetic to a kid, had forced her to choose a life largely without him. By the time he was five, Jack was back with his father above the tavern. But his mother's visits, though infrequent, had always been pleasant and welcome.

However, it would be inaccurate to say that Jack Delaney grew up motherless. In a sense the bar had filled the role. There had been no shortage of women of all ages in all types of roles while growing up at Hank's Place. They collectively mothered him, acted as surrogate aunts, advised him like big sisters, and offered him straight forward friendship. He was even instructed in the ways of a woman. Jack smiled at the thought that his life had not been all bad. He could still smell their perfume and feel their lipstick smeared on his cheeks while they danced him through adolescence into manhood.

Dorothy had taught him the stars saying, "You will always remember me this way." He remembered her tears and her long embrace as she had said the words. He had been eight years old at the time. "Whenever you look up, remember that the Milky Way has a billion stars. I love you more than all the stars in the Milky Way. Don't ever forget that," were the words he still carried in his heart. She had died not long after that in a fall. Some said her new man beat her to death. His mother's absence and then death left a deep painful hole in his heart. He supposed that the widow's death had touched that lonely place.

His truck was backed up against the shed so that he looked out at the house and the driveway. The light was on in Mattie's old room. Anna had decided it was time to move them into her room. He could see her moving back and forth in front of the window. At one point she stopped with arms folded and studied something in the room. Then he watched her open the window and bend down to the screen. "Jack. You out there somewhere?"

"I'm right here. Just hanging out with the dog. I'll be in short-ly," he replied.

"Love you," and she was gone from the window and the light went out. He imagined her crawling under the quilt and twisting and wrapping herself nakedly into the bedding, burrowing into her pillow. Jack had found out the hard way that when she went to sleep it was best to leave her alone. A few late night explorations had put his amorous intentions to an abrupt end.

The gravel drive reflected the half light of the moon through shadowed trees. The breeze ruffled the hair of man and dog, sentinels silent at their posts.

# CHAPTER TWENTY ONE

Most of the spring was spent cleaning up of the Graves farm. As he had done with the Fitzgerald place, Jack began to spruce up the place. There was so much to be done, it was difficult to know where to begin. The house had needed a new roof. Every room on the inside and every square inch on the outside needed paint. The outbuildings were in even sadder shape. Roofs, doors, windows, siding, everything desperately needing attention in every direction and at every turn.

Brush engulfed fence lines surrounded weed choked fields. Neglected machinery collected dust while gears and chains turned to rust. The tractor sat with a dead battery and flat tires, forgotten with an air of abject abandonment. The shed was an old folk's home to the once sturdy line of useful and cared for machines. In dejected silence and lost dignity they waited for the final trip to the junk yard. The farm reminded Jack of a once proud and sturdy man now down at the heels and frail with scuffed shoes and worn clothes hung on a boney frame. Jack had examined everything. The more he looked, the more overwhelmed he became. It would take him years to get it all up to speed. But the house had to come first. Everything else would have to wait.

His days were spent raking the yard, catching the moles that had nearly destroyed it, and trimming all the overgrown vegetation surrounding the house. He unstuck windows, replaced screens, and painted Mattie's bedroom at Anna's request. In addition to all his work, he had been called upon to perform one last job for the widow. As the named executor for Mrs. Fitzgerald, Jack had the responsibility of wrapping up her estate. Her Will had specified that the bulk of her assets were to be sold and the proceeds placed in the hands of the university in order to create a chair in her late husband's name. With sadness, however, Jack learned that her assets were barely enough to cover her debts. The years had simply depleted all her money and she had been forced to borrow against her home.

The beautiful old mansion and the little house next door were to be sold along with its contents. Because it was located by the university and surrounded by student rentals, the price would be depressed. Only those with an interest in converting it to rental apartments had inquired. There would never be a chair in the political science department in the name of Thomas Fitzgerald. Her money was gone and her dream was dead.

Rebecca Moore Fitzgerald had lingered in a coma for two weeks before her death. She never regained consciousness after that last conversation with Jack at the hospital on the day she sent him for Mr. Fitzgerald's picture. Following her explicit instructions, there was no wake or memorial service of any kind. A simple commitment service at grave side had been all that was allowed. It was attended only by Jack, Anna, the funeral director and the minister. Rebecca's only living relative, Tippy Gamble, failed to attend. Her name, age, and date of death, had been all the information provided for the scant obituary except for the mention of the late Mr. Fitzgerald. She was buried next to her husband who had been in the ground for forty years. In the little cemetery at the top of the ridge lay the bodies of the Fitzgeralds, the Graves, Hank Delaney, and Sonny Howland. They were all within one hundred fifty feet of each other.

Mrs. Fitzgerald had remembered Jack in her will to his absolute surprise. She gave him her husband's gun collection as a gesture of good will for his faithful service to her for nearly twenty five years. Unfortunately, most of it had to be sold to help pay her debt. Still, he appreciated the gesture and was happy enough that the widow had remembered him in this way. He had learned over the years that those guns were prized possessions of her husband. For the widow to entrust their care to Jack was an honor which he took seriously. Jack also inherited a box of photos and other mementoes of the widow's life. The lawyer told him to do whatever he wanted with the items. The widow's only living relative, her cousin Tippy Gamble, lived in St. Paul. Rebecca's favorite picture of her husband had been bequeathed to her and Jack was tasked to deliver it when time permitted.

When he found the time, he worked on the Howland murder. The focus had shifted to Mattie's papers as the primary source of additional information. Anna and Jack, mostly Anna, had continued sifting through the voluminous papers. They looked through copies of letters sent and originals of letters received. Journals and poems were read. Then there were the boxes of dated school work, lesson plans, and notes to plow through.

When Anna came across anything that seemed connected, however remotely, she brought it to his attention. So far there had been nothing of value. Although Mattie Graves had been a prolific writer, there had been no further mention about the letters, their origin, their content, or the identity of the author.

Anna had all but abandoned her quest for a master's degree. Instead she worked furiously on her grandmother's papers. Late at night he would find her reviewing them or writing in her journal.

She had taken on the heavy work of examining the written life of Mattie Beret Graves.

Anna divided the school materials and private papers including letters and journals. She read with interest the lesson plan dated August 21, 1950, the day of Sonny Howland's death. As she had previously testified, Mattie's lesson plan for the day had centered on Robert Frost's poems.

In Mattie's beautiful flowing handwriting were the words about how a poem should be written according to Frost. "A poem should begin in delight and end in wisdom."

How many times had she heard her grandmother repeat that line. Anna smiled as she pictured her grandmother gently, but firmly, instructing a room full of farm kids on the nuances of Robert Frost.

At Mattie's wake many former students warmly recalled Mrs. Graves discussing poetry on the first day of school. She had always made the first day fun. It had been Mattie's stated philosophy of teaching that a school year should begin and end to the cadence of a poem. It was her hope that students would leave school a little wiser through the critical use of their minds. But by beginning each year with poetry, Mattie signaled that first and foremost learning should be a joy.

As Anna worked her way into the papers of 1950, she came to the conclusion that Mattie Beret Graves had been a fascinating and interesting woman. All through her written life there were signs of the free spirit that had formed the being of her grandmother. An example of her unwillingness to bend to expectations was found in an exchange of letters between Mattie and Rebecca Fitzgerald about Mattie's patronage of Hank's Place.

Rebecca was appalled that someone with Mattie's class and social standing would frequent a common tavern. Her disapproval was shared by the other ladies in their circle of friends. Mattie's friends from the Third Ward said they were only looking out for her best interest.

Mattie's response was short, elegant, and pointed. First of all, she informed them that she was quite capable of caring for herself. Her friends could do as they pleased. Mattie would go where she wanted and with whom she chose whenever it suited her without permission from her well meaning friends. Before they passed judgment on the good people of Hank's Place, Mattie recommended that they try a Friday night fish fry or a Saturday night dance.

Even though Anna found Mattie's life interesting, not much had been found that would help solve the murder or shine light on the missing letters. Anna had become as obsessed as Jack with solving the murder in which her grandfather had been a suspect. Jack became convinced that Mattie was the key. After finding the poem "Just," written the day of her testimony in Will's trial, he was even surer he was right. There was resolution to the poem. It was as if she would do whatever needed doing.

Everything through December 1950 had been read except for the last few journal entries. All of the school work had been covered as well as all of the letters. Anna had reserved the pleasure of reviewing the final journal entries for 1950 for her 3:00 a.m. coffee break at the Brunswick Café. Anna preferred to keep this time of the night to herself. She did not reciprocate and ask Jack to accompany her to the café. But often he was out wandering the back roads with Harry anyway.

Bud was in back attending to his baking duties upon her arrival. She stuck her head in the door to let him know of her presence then helped herself to a mug of steaming coffee before claiming her spot in the poet's corner.

Sipping her coffee, she looked out at the empty street. At this time of night she basically had the town to herself. She watched as a car parked across the street. Cindy got out and walked towards the café.   Anna wished to be somewhere else, anywhere else, at this given moment.

"Hi Cindy,"  Bud greeted her.

"Hi Bud, I'll take a cup of coffee if you have any made.  High test please," she requested.

Bud poured her a cup of coffee and then went to refill Anna's cup.  He raised his eyebrows in silent communication with her that he recognized the present awkwardness currently filling his little café.   He knew all about Jack and Cindy. After completing his duties, Bud retreated to the back room to continue his baking.  He left the two women to sort out things for themselves.

Neither woman said anything.  Both focused intently on their respective coffee cups and immediate surroundings directly in front of them.  Although each could see the other out of their peripheral vision, not a word was spoken.  Bud returned after a respectable period of time and refilled their cups.

After Bud retreated to the back room, Cindy walked over to Anna's booth and broke the silence.  "It's uncomfortable not to be on a first name basis in such a small community.  I am Cindy Robertson," she extended her hand.

Anna offered her hand as well, "Hi, Anna McCucheon.  Nice to officially meet you.  Would you like to sit down," Anna asked.

"Well, maybe I'll just sit for a moment," Cindy sat down after retrieving her coffee from the counter.

Anna closed her grandmother's journal and sat it to one side.  Settling into the booth, Cindy looked at Anna through wire rimmed glasses.  Cindy wore her soft graying brown hair short. Anna thought her pretty.

"So I hear you have decided to stay on at the farm.  Your grandparents would have been pleased."

"Yes.  I wasn't sure at first, but it seems to be the right thing to do," Anna said.

"I see that you are fixing things up. The new roof makes the house look new."

"Thanks. It will be a long, long process. Everything needs fixing and I mean everything. My grandfather sure let things go in his later years," Anna complained.

"He was such a nice man, your grandfather. Always helped my dad on the farm. Helped everyone else out too. It was so sad to see his mind go at the end."

"Where is your farm," Anna asked.

"Ah, do you know where the old barn stands alone a few miles from your place? The one with the old windmill on the little hill behind it."

"Yes I do," Anna said.

"That's it. After my parents died we let the fire department take down the house for training. It was shot and beyond repair. Then we rented the land to a neighboring farmer," Cindy explained. "We got a lot of pressure from the developers at first, but my brothers and I decided not to sell. I bet you've gotten some pressure too," Cindy added.

"God yes. At first they were relentless. Phone calls, letters, pamphlets, things stuck in my mailbox, some of them even stopped at the farm and stuck offers in my face." Anna grew agitated at the memory. "I just can't stand the thought of anyone else living at the farm. I had to keep it. I hope in the end that I will be able to afford it."

They shared similar feelings about their respective family homesteads and talked awhile in that vein. Bud stuck his head out the door and asked if they needed refills. They waved him off.

Anna asked Cindy about the bar. She said business was slow. In the time she had owned it, she explained she barely kept it in the black. Stricter enforcement of even stricter drunk driving laws had changed the character of tavern drinkers. They drank less at the bar and more at home. She made less. There was little money to be made from the small kitchen. But she had to offer that as an inducement for people to come in and have a few beers. However, she explained to Anna that by doing all the work herself and living above the bar she was able to get by. It did, however, wear on her. Cindy confessed to the idea of turning the place into a convenience store. Anna thought that was a great idea. Cindy wondered if the good people along Stoney Lonesome Road would agree. They were both reluctant to move on to the real subject that sat between them. Neither woman knew exactly what to say in that regard so Cindy finally stood up, again with extended hand and said good night. "I better get going, it's pretty late."

Anna took her hand and thanked her for introducing herself. Cindy hesitated as if she wanted to say something else, but changed her mind. She gathered her things on the counter, bid good night to Bud, and left saying good night to Anna on the way out. Anna watched Cindy get back into her car and drive away.

Anna decided that it was time to explore this with Jack in a little greater detail at the next opportunity. She had only limited observations and a few brief conversations to gauge the relationship between Jack and Cindy. If they were going to make their relationship work, full disclosure and honesty were a must.

It took a while for Anna to regain her equilibrium, finally shaking off the surreal residue of her meeting Cindy. Attempting to refocus, she helped herself to another refill. Anna settled in and returned to Mattie's journal. Mattie's last three entries for the month of December 1950 consisted of two short innocuous passages about nothing of particular importance to anyone and a four stanza poem. As she read the poem Anna first recognized a Frost cadence and rhyme structure.

Mattie's writing was sprinkled throughout with poetry. All of her poetry had Frost overtones which Anna did not find surprising. Not only was Mattie a life long admirer and student of the poet, she was an early member of the Robert Frost Society. So it was to be expected that Mattie would make numerous references to him and would be greatly influenced in her writing by him. Then she read the poem again.

<u>Lovers Creek</u>

Look up to see the moon is crest,
you touch the lace upon my breast.
It sees my soul lost its grace when
again, we meet in lovers nest.

Tho found in our hiding place
no tracks, no trace.
The moon is not the only eye
that finds me here in my disgrace.

Upon his will was need to pry
to catch us in eternal lie.
Tho never just a simple lark
Now it's cause to cry.

Small creek runs through a dismal park.
Stands witness to an act so stark.
Never, ever, to leave a mark.
Breathe no more here in the dark.
Breathe no more here in the dark.

December 31, 1950
Mattie Beret Graves

Anna did not even say goodnight to Bud as she raced for the door. She drove straight home and woke up Jack. After clearing the sleep from his eyes and the cobwebs from his head, he read the poem over several times without comment.

She sat on the bed watching Jack as he leaned up against the headboard, glasses on, intently studying the poem. When he finished he looked up at her and shook his head. "Well, I'll be damned," Jack said with some wonder.

"What do you think," Anna asked.

"I think someone got caught cheating."

"Do you think it was my grandmother," she asked, anxious.

"I don't know. But for damn sure she knew about it. We can at least assume that much. This is about the murder. Look, its setting is Dismal Creek and for sure someone gets killed. It could only be about the murder of Sonny Howland, and she dated it the day he was killed."

They talked until they couldn't keep their eyes open anymore. Then they slept, awakened, and started where they had left off. Coffee and breakfast were had out on the porch. All the while the dissection of the poem continued.

Speculation about Mattie's role narrowed to only a few realistic possibilities. It was a stretch to believe Mattie had simply chronicled a poem about the event with no direct knowledge or participation. More realistically, it appeared that Mattie had direct information about this event.

Anna simply could not come to terms with the idea of her proper grandmother having sex with a man not her husband. Especially with this awful man known as Sonny Howland. It was as difficult picturing her grandmother having this affair as it was for her to try and picture her grandfather killing Sonny Howland. But if she was having an affair with him, it explained the fight in the bar and the murder.

It was first of all clear that Mattie had had significant knowledge of the murder and this affair whether she was directly involved or not. This information was apparently detailed in the missing letters and it was certainly expressed in this new found poem. Furthermore, three people had to be involved. The lovers and the person who discovered them. More importantly, the new motive suggested by the missing letters had been revealed.

For thirty-five years Jack had focused solely on the feud between the Howlands and the Graves as the motive, with Will as the only viable suspect. Now, infidelity had been introduced as a strong motive along with the fact that a third person was most definitely involved in some way. The uncomfortable concern for both of them was who was at the center of the infidelity. As difficult as it was for them to accept, the poem seemed to indicate that Mattie might be that person.

# CHAPTER TWENTY TWO

Jack found Anna sitting in her grandmother's rocking chair. She had positioned it in the alcove and was looking out the window. She was startled out of her reverie by his sudden presence. He had slipped into the room and was leaning against the door jam when she noticed him.

"God Jack, you scared the shit out of me."

He just chucked and smiled.

"You know, I simply can't figure out what to do with this alcove. I've tried a half a dozen arrangements and nothing fits," she said shaking her head, apparently having recovered from her fright.

"Maybe you need to get away from it for a few days. You know, just let it alone for a while. It will come to you," he suggested. "Why don't we go up north for a few days? Get out of the heat. I know I could sure use a break and I know a place we might be able to stay."

"Hmm. Sure. What have you got in mind Jackie boy?"

"A cabin on Lake Superior," Jack said.

"When do we leave?"

It took a few days to make the proper arrangements, but that done, the little family arrived at the resort outside of Washburn. All of the cabins were small and dated, but located on the shore of the biggest fresh water lake in the entire world. A fresh breeze greeted them as the trio went straight from the truck to the water.

Jack led them down a path to a flat rock outcropping that jutted out over the water. Waves broke against the rocks releasing a fine spray that cooled the skin. The temperature next to the lake was ten to fifteen degrees cooler than it was inland and was a welcome relief to the summer heat. The cabin offered a breathtaking view of the lake while maintaining space and privacy. In short, it was paradise.

"How on earth did you ever find this place," Anna asked with obvious delight. Jack explained that a friend on the Sheriff's Department had brought him here years ago. It had been a regular pilgrimage since.

In the morning they went to Washburn for breakfast at the Time Out café. Afterwards, Jack took Anna to Thompson's West End Park to get water. Surrounded by mammoth cottonwood trees, an artesian well pumped ice cold water for all who cared to imbibe. Sitting in the cool of the morning on a flat rock next to the well they looked across the camp site at Lake Superior. It was a calm quiet place respected by campers and locals alike. There was a hushed reverence around this water that had been running steadily for longer than most folks were alive. The sound of the water coming through the long pipe had the power to calm a nervous soul. Harry drank from the runoff pool as Jack described the history of the well.

"It's been running nonstop for over 100 years," he explained. "It was first used for the sawmill. Now anyone who wants to, can stop by for a drink or fill up a container. All of the campers use it and townsfolk too." He showed her how to get a drink of water by holding his hand over the end of the pipe forcing the water up through a drilled hole in the top of the pipe.

"I always drink from the well every time I'm up here. Just think of the thousands of people who have drunk from it over the years. It connects me to all walks of life from all over the world. I like to think that the water has healing power, but if nothing else, it's a damn good drink of water."

Anna agreed that it was indeed a delicious cold drink of water. She couldn't get enough. They filled up the container and returned to the cabin.

Throughout the day that followed, Jack planned his proposal. They drove along Lake Superior to Duluth so that Anna could shop. Jack was learning that patience was the first virtue of a healthy relationship.

Anna seemed free in a way he had not previously observed. It was as though a part of her that she normally reserved to herself was on display. She talked incessantly about everything. On vacation her consumption of weed was truly amazing. Browsing through the Electric Fetus Jack was once again aware of cognitive dissonance. The incongruity of a retired cop cruising the aisles of a head shop with a liberated uptown woman was not lost on him. She bought a tie dyed sun wrap, a pipe for cannabis consumption, incense, and a couple of CDs. With a smile, Jack paid the bill and followed along with his bubble of light.

Scenic Highway 61 North from Duluth offered the lovers a picture of perfection. The old truck purred along at 55 mph as they drove along the shoreline of Lake Superior as far north as Tettegouche State Park. There atop a rocky pine covered outcropping they made love. Far below waves rolled over the rocky beach and broke among the rocks.

Evening found them back in the Canal Park district of Duluth eating Italian and drinking wine. Jack was near drunk and Anna was stoned and drunk. He was having the time of his life. However, he had to admit that there was a certain difference in the energy levels between them. Up to now he felt he had been holding his own. Anna sensed the slight down tick and was not about to call it a night.

"Come on old man, don't run out of gas just yet," she teased, adding "the night's young." Anna slipped off her sandal and played footsie with Jack in a way that was certain to stoke his flagging energy.

"I think I'm going to have a little coffee," Jack motioned for the waiter and ordered for the both of them. "I need a breather from the wine."

After dinner they took a drive in the beautiful night air. The Aerial Lift Bridge connecting the Canal Park district to a long narrow peninsula led to Park Point. They left Old Blue in a small parking lot, then they walked over the boardwalk to the beach. The wind, blowing with some force, carried the mournful loneliness of the big lake. Sky and water line were no longer discernable in the star lit night. The moon was in its full stage, but had not yet risen to cast its ghostly spell on the darkness. It would be up in an hour or so, but for now, it was quite dark.

The lighthouse on the point was warning and welcome across the dark water. Far off the lights of a barge came into view and allowed them to gauge the horizon's distance. To their left down the beach three miles distant were the lights of Duluth. A long curved row of lights defined the shoreline. Nearby where they stood on the beach sea grass whispered in the wind. They took off their shoes and walked across the dunes to the water where they laid upon the beach staring up at the endless night sky.

"My mom told me once that there are a billion stars in the galaxy," he said.

"My dad and I used to do this too. Just lay out in our backyard in Arizona and talk about life. God. I sure miss that. I sure miss him," Anna said.

"Maybe you should visit him."

"Maybe."

Once again she made love to him with the surf nearly reaching where they lay. On their way back to the truck, the moon began to rise. It was well over an hour's drive from Duluth to Washburn and Anna was sound asleep before they crossed the High Bridge back into Wisconsin. Jack drove east with the full moon in his windshield. She lay with her head in his lap. The windows were down and the cool summer night air swirled around the cab. Although they met a few cars, the night belonged to them. Numerous times Jack saw eyes catch the headlights. The biggest danger was a deer crossing the highway, but at a steady 50 M.P.H. he felt pretty safe. At another point a mammoth owl silently crossed his light.

After putting Anna to bed, Jack and Harry went down to the rock. As the full moon cast its white light across the shimmering lake, he listened to water softly lapping the rocks below.

All throughout the day there had been opportunities to ask for Anna's hand. At each juncture, Jack passed up the chance. The gap in their age had been on display today. While Anna had gotten a second wind, Jack ran out of gas. Without a fortuitous nap snatched while Anna had shopped yet again on the way back from Tettegouche Park, Jack would never have made it through the day. This did not bode well for the long run of their lives. Jack was 55 years old and Anna was 36. He realized that when she was his age, he would already be in his 70s. It was not a stretch to think that he might not be able to keep up over the long haul. The pace was more natural with Cindy, he had to admit.

It was also a fact of life that Cindy was always present and sat between them. In a way, it seemed wrong to take this final step with Anna without first looking Cindy in the eye and telling her that it was finally over between them. Maybe there was a small nagging voice that questioned whether it was indeed over with Cindy and that is what kept him from proposing marriage to Anna

McCucheon. Shaking his head in frustration, Jack returned to the cabin.

When Jack awoke he could smell coffee. He found Anna wrapped in a blanket on the rock watching the sun rise. Shortly after joining her, the owner of the resort showed up along the bank with a set of bagpipes.

"Good morning to ya," he called down to them.

"Morning," Jack replied. Anna waved.

"Would you mind if I play to the Lake? It's a ritual of sorts."

"Not at all," Anna said. "Please play."

So as the sun rose over the big lake, he played "Amazing Grace" to the dawn. As the familiar notes drifted across the lake, the two lovers huddled together under the blanket sipping coffee and holding hands.

Later over pancakes at the Time Out café, Anna observed that it seemed like they were in some kind of fairy tale. Although Jack certainly agreed, he also knew the long weekend had exposed his lingering doubts about their age difference. All of his life he had been cautious and there was no reason to change now. The marriage proposal would have to wait until the doubts were satisfied.

On their way home they again stopped to drink from the artesian well. The trip south took four hours under normal conditions. As it was, they did not arrive back on the farm until well after dark. Taking the back way they explored little parks, poked around curiosity shops, ate, and made love twice along the remote roads. It had truly been a great time.

Once again, they settled into their routine of repairing the old place. Anna resumed her work on her grandmother's papers while Jack worked on the house repair and the case. But as they discussed the case theory in light of the "new" evidence, an unfortunate tension arose between them. Anna became increasingly defensive of her grandparents. The "Lovers Creek" poem had opened a Pandora's Box of uncomfortable possibilities to which

Anna couldn't subscribe. It thwarted an open discussion of the poem and its implications, frustrating Jack.

Slowly, imperceptibly, a storm began to gather in the little house along Stoney Lonesome Road.

# CHAPTER TWENTY THREE

Anna watched the lingering sunset over the Rockies. The plane's westward progress slowed the reddening sky's descent into darkness. When, finally, the skyline faded to a dim reddish glow she settled back into her seat. The sunset flight to Phoenix was only half full and Anna had the row of seats to herself.

The pit in her stomach grew each time she thought about the argument she had had with Jack. The more they talked about her grandmother's possible involvement in the murder, the deeper their disagreement became. Jack had grown convinced that a love triangle explained the murder.

As he explained his theory to her, "Look, it all makes sense. Will caught them together at the creek and killed Howland. Mattie lied for them both at the trial. And," he added with emphasis "the poem she wrote the day of the trial seems to confirm that she was doing simply what she had to do." He went on to add "only Mattie's involvement would explain Will's actions. If his wife was not involved, why would he kill a man?"

"I don't care how much sense it makes or how neat and tidy it is, my grandmother would never have been involved with Sonny Howland. Never," Anna challenged. Their conversation seesawed back and forth until it escalated into a shouting match. Jack took Harry and left. She had not heard from him in over a week.

Anna could accept the notion that her grandfather may have killed Sonny Howland. It seemed to Anna like the man probably deserved it. Maybe they met at the creek to finish the fight started at the bar, she thought further. But any thoughts that Grams was involved with Sonny Howland, were repugnant. It was her core rejection of such a thought that led to the fight with Jack.

"Okay, okay," she had defiantly said to Jack, "my grandmother was not a saint. She was capable of seeing another man. Of course, that's possible. But I will never, ever, believe that it was with that creep." Her conclusion on this point prompted Jack to ask the obvious question. "So who was it then?"

Jack then attempted to explain that Sonny Howland was big, athletic and good looking. His wavy brown hair was worn combed straight back in the fashion of the day. Light on his feet, he was an excellent dancer and had a reputation as a charmer. Besides, Jack said "women like to be around a man with a dangerous streak. Being close to the flame gives them a thrill. Where do you think cop groupies come from?" That had been more than Anna could take in one setting. First, she challenged him on his "extensive" knowledge of women in general. Then Anna drug Cindy into the argument. If he was such an expert, how was it that he had managed his relationship with Cindy so well, she had said sarcastically. By the way, she had wanted to know, just what the "exact" nature of that relationship was. It was at this particular point that Jack had left.

During the run up to the argument's finale, Jack had suggested they make an all out effort to find the letters, starting with her father. He pointed out that John was the only one in the position to take them, his previous denials notwithstanding. Although Anna had defended her father, deep down she knew that Jack was right. It was a loose end that had gnawed on her as well, although she never admitted that to Jack. So she called her dad, booked her ticket, and boarded the plane for Phoenix.

A sea of lights greeted Anna as they approached on their landing. "Welcome to Sky Harbor International Airport. The time is 10:45 p.m. Air temperature is 95 degrees. Enjoy your stay." Home had never looked so good.

Anna spotted her father's bald head above the crowd around the baggage carousel. He appeared to be the same fit, thin, tan, and casually academic man she had last seen at her grandmother's funeral. His disposition seemed improved, however. John Graves always looked happier when farthest away from Stoney Lonesome Road.

"Father," she wrapped herself around his tall frame.

"How was your flight," he asked, reciprocating her physical embrace with a long squeeze of his own. Holding her by the shoulders at arms length, father eyed daughter for a hint of why she had made the visit. Finding none, he said "it sure is good to see you, welcome home. Come on, let's get your bags." With initial appraisals of each other complete the two caught up on the latest as they retrieved her bags and drove home.

They took their lemonade on the open sided back patio. Lights from the pool cast a soft aqua light on the backyard. The enveloping heat felt familiar and secure. Anna was thankful for the absence of mosquitoes which were the ruin of many Wisconsin summer nights.

Temperature at pool side was 98 degrees and it was expected to reach 115 degrees the next day. After catching up on all the safe subjects, Anna told her father about her relationship with Jack and its latest negative turn. While she told her father that an argument had prompted her return home, Anna did not reveal the subject of the argument itself, nor did she reveal the purpose of her visit. Her father was attentive and sympathetic to Anna's relationship woes. He had always listened to her problems with patience and understanding.

Retired from Arizona State University, John Graves lived quietly among his books and his lush backyard garden. Fragrant and brightly colored foliage graced one's senses everywhere in the backyard. Paving steps wound through flowers, shrubs, olive and eucalyptus trees, and water features. Benches and chimes invited a person to sit and ponder.

While John gardened away his private hours, he had spent his professional life in pursuit of knowledge. Arizona academia had been his life. Students enjoyed his style and teaching assistants competed for available positions under his tutelage. He taught courses on Abraham Lincoln that had been described by students as "almost poetic". John Graves looked every inch the professor and was well liked and respected. Often he paraphrased his hero Lincoln joking that he was as thin as the shadow of a starving bird. John also looked nothing like Will Graves.

Anna favored her father's thin frame, green eyes, and studious nature. "Happy to be home," John asked over a sip of lemonade. Anna was stretched out on the chaise looking up at the stars. "Feels great," she said while looking at the North Star.

"What do you think it all means, Dad? It's all so beautiful, so.... so, words can't describe how it makes me feel." They had always had philosophical discussions about the meaning of life and everything else. Neither had a well defined notion, however. Both sensed the mystical beauty of it all and their shared connection to it.

"It is a serious undertaking, you know. Trying to find out the meaning of life. I've heard that it consumes some people. It takes over their lives. Becomes an obsession. You might even know someone like that," John said in a self deprecating tone. Anna smiled, thinking of her father's obsession with Abraham Lincoln.

"Anna," John asked after several moments of silence. No answer. Smiling to himself, John covered up his daughter with a light blanket and went to bed.

# CHAPTER TWENTY FOUR

Anna's stay coincided with the ever increasing temperature of an Arizona summer. It was so hot during the day that it actually made her eyeballs hurt. A quick dash into the supermarket turned the car into an oven. Even the blacktopped parking lot seemed sticky to the feet. But Anna enjoyed every minute.

Most of her time was spent alternating between dips in the pool and baking in the sun. When her father went to the university for various reasons, Anna sunbathed in the nude. It made her feel exceedingly naughty and liberated. A phone call to an old girlfriend produced invitations to shopping and partying with her old crowd. Arizona felt safe. As a result, a serious soul-searching began regarding her relationship with Jack and whether returning to Wisconsin was the right thing to do.

The space afforded by her trip to Arizona gave Anna perspective on her relationship with Jack. That she loved him was not in doubt. She thought him to be a wonderful man. Reluctantly however, she had begun to think about their age gap as a liability. He constantly referred to things from memory that she only knew as history. His childhood and young adult stories sounded much like those of her parents.

Music from Jack's era was alright and some of it was even great she thought, but it really wasn't her choice. Occasionally Jack would turn up the truck radio to Elvis or Johnny Cash. She preferred the blues.

Where Anna was perpetually connected to the world by cell phone and the internet, Jack kept his cell phone off except for emergencies and did not own a computer. It was also clear that Jack had entered middle age, displaying his lack of energy at times.

On different occasions during their trip north she felt he was about to propose, but nothing had been forthcoming. If he had asked, she probably would have said yes. Indeed, if he called this minute and asked, Anna knew she would be on the next plane home. But she hadn't heard a word since he walked out the door.

No matter what her final decision turned out to be, she had come to Arizona with a particular purpose in mind. It was that purpose that she intended to carry out, so it was time that she asked her father about the letters.

There was no better place to discuss serious business, or any other kind of business, than at Rustler's Rooste. It was Anna and her father's favorite restaurant in Phoenix. Located half way up the mountain it overlooked the valley floor. Planes from Sky Harbor could be seen landing and taking off. The setting sun reflected off the buildings of downtown Phoenix. Her favorite time to visit Rustler's Rooste was at dusk.

They left the car with the valet and then walked passed Horny, the long-horned steer penned up outside the door. Western clad waiters and waitresses served beer in pint jars on red and white checked tablecloths. John and Anna went out to the wrap around deck and stood at the rail overlooking the Valley of the Sun. As dusk faded towards night, the lights of the valley began to wink on. For as far as they could see in either direction the valley became awash in twinkling lights.

"I love this view. It's absolutely my favorite," Anna said as she viewed the scene from the deck. "I could stand here forever." Below them on the gravel patio they watched a wedding party gather for what appeared to be the rehearsal dinner. Tiny white lights outlined the terrace and wood smoke from an open pit lent a Western air to the festive setting. Inside, they could hear the western band tuning up.

"Come on, let's eat," John put his arm around his daughter and guided her back into the restaurant. Basically, the upstairs of Rustler's Rooste is the watering hole for patrons waiting for the dinner call. The downstairs eating area is accessed by stairs or by a slide. Young and old alike often take the slide. John and Anna never failed to exercise that particular option. Her mother had always thought they were both nuts and refused to use the slide, much preferring the stairs.

Western decor, western clad waiters and waitresses, mounted rattlesnakes, western music and a western menu greeted John and Anna at the bottom of the slide. The cattleman's special was accompanied by the ringing of the dinner bell. It rang as the food was brought to those who had ordered that particular specialty. Rustler's Rooste never failed to give Anna a good feeling no matter the occasion.

Feasting on barbeque ribs, spuds, cowboy beans, and sweet corn they talked and drank. Licking off their sauce covered fingers, they washed down their food with pints of cold Coors. Although Anna dearly wanted to ask about the letters, it was not the time.

Instead of zeroing in on the letters, Anna steered the conversation towards her grandmother's life in general. After all, she was genuinely interested. As she explained to her dad "she seems so real to me now. Almost more than when she was alive." John was filled in on his daughter's recent study of Mattie's papers.

"Why all the interest," he asked.

"I don't really know. I just can't get enough of her." This was the truth, but she left out the attempt to solve the murders as a specific motivation. John did not delve deeper into Anna's reason for the interest, seemingly satisfied with his daughter's explanation.

"Tell me something I don't know about her life," she prompted. "Surprise me."

"Well, I don't know. Let's see. How about Kennedy's inaugural?"

"The only thing I know is that you went there with Grams. She always liked to show me the picture that was taken with the two of you standing in front of the Capitol. But I have never heard the details."

"She took me to Washington, D.C. in January of 1961 to see the inauguration of President John F. Kennedy," he began.

John described how he had never seen his mother so nervous and excited as she waited for her invitation to the inauguration. It arrived by regular mail on a Saturday. John went to get the mail following chores while his dad went into the house. His mother had been expecting the letter and had looked for it every day during the previous week. John was just as excited as she was to receive the letter.

He raced into the house and proudly handed her the envelope. Mattie wiped her hands on the dish towel and gingerly took the letter from her son. Its return address was from Inaugural Headquarters. Embossed lettering and the inaugural seal made it the most official document ever to arrive at the Graves farm. Will, in his usual place by the stove, put down his western and watched his wife open the invitation. She read out loud that the honor of her presence for the inauguration of John Fitzgerald Kennedy was requested. Will smiled at Mattie and winked at John.

"Are you going to go," Will teased.

It had all started when Mattie volunteered to help organize teas during the Wisconsin primary. Because of her family's connections, Mattie was instrumental in setting up get-togethers, or "teas" as the Kennedys preferred to call them, in various homes in and around Brunswick. For her efforts, she was invited to the inauguration and ball. The invitation was addressed to Mrs. Will Graves and guest. It turned out that the guest would be John Graves, her thirteen year old son.

By choice and necessity, Will had previously decided not to attend. There was no one else to milk the cows and his interest in politics was small. Although he was squarely behind Senator Kennedy, he had no interest in active participation, leaving that to his wife. When Mattie came home from the last tea she had reported Eunice Kennedy's promise that when "Jack won, they would love to have her come to Washington for the ball." Will suggested that she take John instead. Besides, John had an interest in all that "baloney" and would enjoy the "hullabaloo." So they agreed that John would watch the 35th President of the United States take the oath of office in Washington, D.C.

Brushing up against the elegance of the Kennedy clan and bearing witness to history was not all that was in store for Mattie Graves. No sooner had the invitation arrived when she got a phone call from the National Robert Frost Society. Because Frost would be in D.C. to read at the inaugural, a small luncheon had been planned for select society members. They wanted to know if it was possible for her to attend. Mercury himself could not have responded faster.

Never was more fuss made over anything in the Graves household following that blissful day of invitation. Mattie spent more money on clothes for the various events than she normally budgeted for two years. She went into serious consultation with her friends from the Third Ward, especially Mrs. Fitzgerald. Fashion magazines were bought and scoured for ideas. Every scrap of information regarding inaugural protocol was consumed. No stone unturned. Even young John was turned out in fitting style. Will smiled, shook his head, and commented on the run away train.

But the effort was worth it. Although Mattie was in her early forties, she still retained the beauty and charm of her youth. She was in her last bloom. John remembered how President Kennedy brightened noticeably while exchanging pleasantries with Mattie. Mrs. Kennedy was the most beautiful thing he had ever seen.

Clear cold January air greeted the multitudes who had gathered to watch the inauguration. John sat with his mother in the bright sunshine as the young President "let the word go forth from this time and place that the torch has been passed to a new generation of Americans." He and his mother were particularly stirred by the new President's challenge that all Americans had a duty to contribute to the country's well-being, not just take from it. They had both been moved by his eloquence. John always ranked Kennedy's inaugural along with Lincoln's "with malice toward none" second.

John thought that his mother had been nearly as excited about the presence of Robert Frost. Mattie expressed embarrassment for the old poet when he was unable to read the poem he had written for the occasion due to the sun's glare. She was relieved when he was able to recite a different poem from memory which fit the occasion. The entire event was wonderful. However, Mattie could not hide her disappointment that she had been unable to meet Robert Frost. When they had excitedly gathered for the luncheon, the poet laureate sent word that he was unable to attend due to his other inaugural duties.

By the time John had finished the story, they had finished eating and decided to adjourn over coffee. After retrieving the car from the valet, they drove to the Tempe House near campus. Two mugs of cream laden rich coffee were taken to a dimly lit corner table. Candles flickered and incense burned in and around murmured conversations. Academic types mixed seamlessly with tattooed and pierced twenty-some-things. Lovers huddled. Friends talked. Here and there a muttered "Fuck" or laugh could be heard above the muted chatter. In the midst of it all, a serious conversation was developing between father and daughter.

"Dad, I need to ask you something," Anna said tentatively. John looked at his daughter over his glasses with raised eyebrows.

"Okay," he responded in kind. She fidgeted in her chair and mindlessly moved the coffee cup, creamer, spoon, and napkins around on the table in a haphazard re-arrangement, all the time averting her eyes from her father. Having reached the point of her trip, Anna created this momentary delay. It was as if she suddenly had second thoughts. But taking a deep breath, she looked up at her father and plunged ahead.

"What can you tell me about the murder of Sonny Howland?"

"I was wondering when you would get around to asking me about this. It was inevitable that you would cross paths with this aspect of our lives living up there at the farm. What do you want to know?"

Her first question was why he or her grandparents had never said one word to her about such a huge aspect of the Graves legacy. Although she understood that it was obviously an embarrassment to the family. First of all, just being involved in any way in something as sordid as a murder cast long shadows. But, to be the accused - even if cleared - how awful. Shouldn't she have been told anyway?

John explained that the family simply did not talk about it at all, ever. When John learned about it at school he naturally asked Will and Mattie. Both sat him down at the kitchen table and in no uncertain terms told him that Will Graves did not kill Sonny Howland. Nor did he have any involvement of any kind. That was the truth no matter what anyone said. Furthermore, the topic was never to be brought up again. "Case closed," Mattie had said at the time.

"Is that why you came all the way out here, just to test my memory about an old unsolved murder," he asked.

"Well," she paused. "There is the matter of the missing letters," she admitted. "Grams wrote me that the letters contained some awful secret. The second I mentioned it to Jack he thought the letters had to be about the murder. But it makes no sense for

Grams to tell me about them and then not give them to me. Jack believes someone took them to protect whoever was involved in the murder."

Anna then filled her dad in on the poems and the real reason for the argument with Jack. It had become quite clear that Mattie had to have had some knowledge of some kind. Everything had pointed in that direction. She delicately broached the subject of infidelity. Reaching into her purse Anna brought out Mattie's letter with a p.s. about the secret pain, the poems "Just" and "Lovers Creek."

Her father read the three documents all written in his mother's beautiful flowing hand. Silently he reread them again. It was obvious to Anna that treading over this ground caused him a certain amount of distress. At times he rubbed his forehead and at others he bit his lip. The color had left his face. Finally, he put them aside and looked up at Anna.

"The missing letters are not about the murder," he said quietly. "Those letters say nothing whatsoever about the murder of Sonny Howland."

"How would you know that?"

"I've known about the letters for forty years. Mother kept them in her secret compartment in her writing desk. I was snooping around her things, actually looking to find a couple of cigarettes, when I found them. When she died I removed them from the drawer. I thought it was time to close that chapter. I am sorry I lied to you; I just wanted to protect you. That's all."

They decided to continue the conversation at the house and rode in silence on the way home. Although Anna had a million questions, she let her dad off the hook for the night. He begged off until morning citing fatigue. To Anna it was the first time her father had looked old.

# CHAPTER TWENTY FIVE

"Morning," John said from his chaise lounge patio chair. Anna shuffled by with her coffee and sleepily snuggled into her place. She had slept quite late. Allowing sufficient time for sleep to clear from his daughter's mind, John continued the previous evening's conversation. He had been waiting for her to get up.

"I'll talk. You listen. Deal?"

"Deal," she agreed.

"I was 15 years old when I went into my mother's room to look for cigarettes. Mother and Dad had gone up town for something and as usual I stayed at home. I snooped around for a while but couldn't find where she hid them. By accident I found the hidden drawer in her writing desk. Sure enough, I found the cigarettes. The letters, three of them, were tucked away down in the back of her secret compartment. At first I didn't look at them, but curiosity got the better of me so I went ahead. As God as my witness I wish I had never seen the damn things." For a time John remained quiet. Anna said nothing, giving her father the space he needed to tell the story. She refilled their cups before he continued.

"They were all addressed to my mother and had been delivered to her school. All were unsigned, but were written in the same strong hand. Obviously by a man. The envelopes were dated. The first one was in 1945. The second in 1947, the year I was born, and the third in 1950."

"Essentially, they were love letters. It was a man pleading with a woman to accept his love and not turn away. The clear implication was that this man was my father." Anna gasped, but said nothing, sitting with her arms crisscrossing her chest as if to hold in the emotion that was plainly showing on her face.

"They were all postmarked from St. Paul, but other than that, there were no distinguishing or identifying characteristics about the letters themselves. I must have been so engrossed in them that I did not hear my parents come home. My first warning was the closing of the porch door. I quickly put them away and got out of the bedroom as fast as I could. I was no more than into the hall-way when Mother made it to the top of the stairs. She didn't catch me, but she was suspicious enough to ask what I had been up to or if I had been in her bedroom. I must have looked awfully guilty.

I lied. Boy, did I lie. Mother gave me a look I'll never, ever for-get. Without having to say so, I knew that if I got caught lying or snooping, she'd have my head. I also knew I could never ask her about the letters or the true identity of my father." Almost as an aside he added "by the way, your grandfather, Will, was always and will remain my father. Doesn't matter if it's biological or not." He informed Anna that Will had always been good to him over the years even if he was remote. There was no way for John to know if Will knew the truth. By his actions toward him he never said or did anything that gave that particular piece of information away. But a discovery of that kind would rock anyone. Its weight left young John confused, angry, and frustrated. All causes of his life's ambition to avoid Stoney Lonesome Road.

They resumed a normal conversation of give and take once the weight of the truth had been lifted from John's shoulders by his confession. She could see that her father was in a fragile state of mind after unburdening himself. The only other person John had told was his wife, and she had taken the secret to her grave.

Through gentle probing Anna learned that John had retrieved the three letters before the funeral and burned them once he got back to Arizona. He had intended to shield Anna from this ugly family tale. His desire was to have the story end with him so that she would not be burdened by its weight.

Two things of great import came out of the post-confessional conversation. To Anna's immense relief, her father was clear about one thing for certain. Sonny Howland was not his father. Early on, John wondered about this possibility when he learned of the murder. However, doing some amateur investigation of his own, he realized that the first two letters were written while Sonny Howland was in prison. Besides, that would have been so out of character for Mattie Graves as to be implausible. Secondly, the letters contained nothing about the murder itself. They revealed infidelity and illegitimacy. That had been Mattie's secret pain. Not a whiff or hint about murder was in the letters.

Although it was great to have the mystery solved about the missing letters, it was frustrating not to have solved the murder. Additionally, she now had the burden of knowing that her grandmother had cheated on her grandfather and that her grandfather was not really her grandfather. Further, she had no way of knowing the identity of her real grandfather. It was also a little hard to swallow that her revered grandmother had carried on a long term affair. It appeared that every conundrum had a catch at the point of solvability.

# CHAPTER TWENTY SIX

A few days after he heard that Anna returned to Arizona, Jack went out to the farm to pick up his things. There was a note on the kitchen table asking him to keep an eye on the place while she was away. So Jack watered her plants, mowed the lawn, and picked up her mail. He did not stay there; however, it just didn't seem right.

The little cottage again served as home to Jack and Harry. No one had bought the place yet. Since he was executor of the will, it was his prerogative to stay. An estate company had been hired to dispose of the personal property. The date had been set for the auction to rid the estate of its remaining items. Anything left after that would be given to Goodwill or thrown away. Once the personal property was gone, the real estate would be auctioned to the public. A private gun collector had purchased the valuable guns from the estate. All that remained were a few old hunting guns and a nice gun cabinet which was promised to Jack.

On his last visit to the farm Jack noticed ripening black caps. The small black berries were sweet and excellent for pies. This trip he decided to pick a few. Not far from the Graves place he walked up the ancient field road that paralleled Dismal Creek. It was early in the day and still cool enough to be comfortable. As Jack walked slowly along the trail, he picked and ate while filling the five quart ice cream bucket he kept in the pickup for just such an occasion. Full, ripe, and sweet, the fruit stained his fingers and satisfied his pallet. A light breeze ruffled the sumacs and water gurgled in the creek. Bird songs serenaded Jack and Harry as they left their trail in the dew covered grass. He had to first spray himself down with insect repellant or the mosquitos would have carried him off.

As Jack wandered along picking black caps on this perfect summer morning, time merged and disappeared into a simple rhythm. Before Jack realized it, he found himself below the windmill on Cindy's old farmstead. He walked up the hill to pick the berries he knew would be there—Cindy would not mind. Indeed, blackberry bushes choked the knob of the hill. Trees had grown up through the mill stand and nearly reached the fan. Although the mill no longer pumped water, its useful purposes were far from over. Turning and creaking in the wind it served as a useful reminder of the past. Jack remembered making love to Cindy on this very spot.

He had deliberately stayed away from Hank's Place and Cindy, knowing he was vulnerable from his fight with Anna. Jack was unsure what he would do if Cindy gave him the "come hither." But now he had created a conundrum by picking the fruit. Cindy had always taken care of his berries.

Auction time at the widow Fitzgerald's arrived. Curiosity seekers, antique dealers, and serial auction attendees made for a large assembly. Long before they opened for business, people began showing up. Many tried to buy early what they would have to bid for later. No amount of dissuasion could deter them. They wandered all over the property, in and out of the house, around the grounds, pawing, looking, and commenting under their breath. Mostly he ignored the crowd by staying in his little house.

But as luck, chance, or fate would have it, Jack was "needed" to answer a few questions about items for sale. It was absolutely "necessary" that he be available for the sale of the real estate because of his intimate knowledge of the property. Telling Harry to "stay" Jack followed the very professional auctioneer's assistant to the front yard by the big house. He watched the auctioneer work the crowd from a raised platform. "Who will give me a fifty-dollar bid, do I hear a bid, you sir will you give me a fifty-dollar bill for this lamp." The auctioneer turned towards Jack and said "it works, don't it," drawing a laugh from the crowd. The auctioneer received an affirmative nod and away he went. Of course, while Jack was enjoying the patter of the auctioneer, Cindy walked up and said hello.

There was not much else to do except ask her if she wanted a cup of coffee. They walked to the concession stand and stood in a short line while a mother ordered a hot dog for a small boy who was standing on his tiptoes trying to see into the small trailer.

"I love auctions. I don't know why, I just do," Cindy said in a way that implied the "auction" was the reason for her presence. "Coffee and donuts. They taste better at an auction than anywhere else. I should know," she laughed and patted her bottom.

They took their food over by the fence and focused on the task of eating while commenting on the crowd. From time to time they nodded or waved to people they'd both been around most of their lives. Neighbors passing by did not seem surprised seeing them together. For most folks, Jack and Cindy were a couple. After all, they had been together off and on since childhood.

When they were no longer encumbered by food or diverted by passers-by, they got around to the fact that Jack had moved off the farm. Neighborhood secrets are hard kept in a country bar. Most information found its way to Hank's Place sooner or later. Before long, the story was out that Anna had flown off to Arizona and Jack had moved home to his little cottage.

"Everything okay Jack," Cindy asked, touching his arm in that way she always did out of concern.

"Well, you know. Heard huh," he said and looked down. In the background the auctioneer could be heard selling off the widow's possessions.

"Where will you go when you sell the place," Cindy wanted to know.

"Not sure. Hadn't thought about it much. I'm kind of surprised to be back here in the first place to tell you the truth." Then, changing the subject, he told Cindy about the berries. As always, Cindy volunteered to make his pies if he brought them by. Maybe he could stop in on Sunday morning she suggested. Hank's Place was no longer open on Sundays, she said. Before he knew it, Jack agreed to stop by at 10 o'clock for coffee.

Then it was time to sell the house. A company that operated Bed and Breakfasts beat out a student rental landlord for the highest bid on the property. This pleased Jack to no end. It made him very happy to know that the place would be maintained properly and not succumb to student rental shabbiness. The only downside was that the closing would take place in thirty days. Within a month Jack would need to find a new place to live. His world of possibilities had grown considerably smaller in a short period of time.

At the appointed time, Harry and Jack arrived at Cindy's back door on Sunday morning. An exterior stairway led to the second floor apartment above the tavern, which looked forlorn and abandoned. Having been there before, Harry bounded up the steps three at a time, while Jack purposefully took his time.

Met on the stairs by the smell of frying bacon and at the screen door by a "come on in," Jack wondered if this was such a good idea.

Cindy took the berries and put them on the counter as she told him to "help yourself to some coffee." He retrieved "his" cup from the cupboard and filled the mug, noticing that she'd prepared his favorite breakfast.

They sat facing each other at the small two person kitchen table under the window. They alternated looking at each other while eating breakfast. Harry was literally at their feet with his tail resting on Cindy's feet and his head on Jack's. The same scenario had played itself out so many times before that it was more familiar than awkward, considering the circumstances. The shabby furniture belonging to his father had been replaced by Cindy's serviceable pieces. Fresh flowers adorned the freshly painted and newly wallpapered apartment. The interior of this small living space contrasted sharply with the general dreariness of the exterior and grounds.

He had toyed with the idea of moving in with her over the years. However, once Cindy moved above the tavern, all possibility of that had ended. Under no circumstances would Jack Delaney move back into the bar. There had never been talk of Cindy moving into the little cottage. The widow would have frowned upon such an arrangement. But Jack had spent enough nights in Cindy's bed for the mornings to have become routine.

He was quite aware, now that he was in her lair, that he had little control over his willpower. This was especially so when Cindy opened herself to him. Throughout the years of waxing and waning, of closing and opening, there were times when she was irresistible. There was a smoldering animal sexuality in her eyes. He knew as they finished their coffee that if he did not leave at once, Cindy would be at him in the back bedroom.

A big part of him wanted to go to the back room. His need for comfort rose within him like a wave and no one had ever provided the balm for those needs like Cindy. It was, he supposed, her greatest hold upon him and her greatest gift.

She massaged his soul with her welcoming warm presence. In her current state, Cindy bloomed like a flower. This was not lost on Jack as he looked across the table at Cindy, watching her eyes flare as she talked. Her dusky voice grew sexier in this mood. When she responded to his remarks with "you devil" he knew he was in trouble.

Before it was too late, he got up to leave. Cindy cut him off at the door and kissed him long and passionate. She moved against him and he felt himself respond. Thank God for Harry who got between their legs demanding attention.

Unlocking from the embrace, Jack laughed at Harry. Even Cindy, who did not want anything to come between them at the moment, couldn't resist the big dog. With that, the spell was broken and Jack made his escape. Cindy promised to call him when the pies were ready. At the door he paused and offered a tentative thanks. Cindy smiled, but the crestfallen look on her face gave away the disappointment registered in her heart. Reaching out in that way of hers, she said "I had to try."

"I guess I had to let you," Jack said. Then he turned and walked down the steps. As he did so, Jack felt Cindy's eyes on his back, burning with sadness and longing.

# CHAPTER TWENTY SEVEN

Sally cowered in a corner as Doyle broke everything in his path. She was half clad and bleeding from her nose and mouth, whimpering. Doyle unleashed his wrath on Sally before turning it on the apartment.

The cops had already been called from the bar on the first floor just below Sally's place. Although it was not unusual to hear a ruckus when Doyle was around, this time it was different. All of the old-timers later agreed that this time it sounded like he was killing her. They sat huddled together sipping their beer while looking up at the ceiling with their watery eyes. More than one squad had been dispatched.

All reason escaped Doyle the moment Sally informed him that Anna had gone back to Arizona. She had heard the information through the beautician grape vine. Accusing her of lying to piss him off, he pounded her with his prosthetics. When she swore that she was telling the truth, he beat her some more.

What Sally didn't know was that Doyle had been ready to execute his plan to kill Anna when he received the news. Night after night he finalized everything as he watched from his perch in the graveyard. Doyle had not worried when Anna initially left the farm because she often left for days at a time. But he never imagined she had gone back to Arizona for good.

Although as time went on, he began to suspect that something was wrong. Jack came and went, but he did not stay either. The little house remained dark each night. Inexorably, the pressure began to build as his frustration mounted.

So when Sally finally told him what she had heard, it was confirmation rather than revelation. Her words removed the cork from the bottle and Doyle erupted in a spasm of molten hate. His carefully laid out plan to kill Anna and himself had been defeated. That he was once again denied justice was more than he could take. Sally was simply in his path.

Above the breaking glass, crashing furniture, and his own ranting he heard the sirens. There was no doubt jail would follow. It was time to go.

The capstone to the night of destruction was a final boot to Sally's face. As Sally sank into oblivion, Doyle crunched his way across broken glass and out the door leaving it open. With smoke belching and engine roaring, the old caddy spewed gravel and swayed out onto the street. When Doyle hit the edge of town the broken speedometer would have registered over 100 had it been working. The chase was on.

With the Letterman monologue over, Harry and Jack hit the road for a little patrol. Following his usual practice, Jack left his cell phone in the glove compartment and his gun at home. He did not own a police scanner. It was a typical late September night with cool air flowing through the truck's cab signaling that fall was in the air. Harry was at his place on the passenger's side with the wind in his face.

Tonight's patrol was particularly aimless. His drift over the back roads resembled his state of mind. A restless lack of focus had tenaciously settled upon him. First he went this way, then that. He found himself going in circles crossing the same intersection two and three times. At times he lacked the concentration to remember the road he was on. His mind was elsewhere. Arizona to be precise.

Eventually Jack and Harry looped and turned, drove and drifted, until they came upon Stoney Lonesome Road. He was drawn to the very place he wanted to avoid. At the corner sat a closed and forlorn looking Hank's Place. Low level lights from coolers and beer signs faintly lit the interior.

The light was on over the back stairs to Cindy's apartment and Cindy's car was gone. It was after closing time and he wondered if she had taken her brother home again. Father Dan often drank more than the law allowed. She refused to let him drive in that condition. Everyone overlooked the fact that Father Dan was an alcoholic because of his wonderful spirit. He ended each mass with the words, "Don't forget, a little grace goes a long ways. Now go out there and be nice to people."

Approaching his favorite view of the valley, that point where Stoney Lonesome Road tops out then curves down into the valley, Jack slowed as always. He would have slowed even if he had known for sure there was nothing around the bend. It was a habit born out of the car crash with Cindy. Habit also made him cautious enough to pay attention as he rounded the corner.

Whatever the source of his vigilance, on this night it saved his life. As Jack came around the corner his headlights picked up the glint of metal moving fast. Born with quick reflexes, he jerked the truck into the ditch barely missing the car which roared by him up the hill. The caddy did not have its headlights on, but Jack saw enough to know that it belonged to Doyle Howland. Struggling to keep the truck under control on the steep bank was a lost cause. Old Blue turned on its side and came to rest up against a tree.

Harry yelped as Jack ended up on top of the big dog. The night was quiet except for the ticking of the stalled engine, the fading sound of the rusted old caddy, and a siren approaching in the distance. Then everything went black.

He awoke to the sterility of the critical care unit. Monitors, muffled voices, and muted lighting mixed to form a surreal reality. Jack had been here many times escorting the battered, the bruised, and the broken to this place. But, from his vantage point in the hospital bed, it felt new. Always before he was the observer to the process, now he was the patient.

Then the memory of the accident hit him like a train. Feeling a frantic urge to find out about Harry, he attempted to sit up. A blinding stab of pain caused him to call out, bringing the nurse on the run. All Jack could see was a field of red and the black specks that accompany approaching unconsciousness. The nurse and then the doctor were all over him, checking equipment, talking to him, flipping charts, and adjusting his medication. Then blackness came as he thought he heard Harry yelp again and again and again and again.

When next he awoke, the sheriff was standing next to his bed.

"Howdy Bub," Red Slade nodded approvingly at him.

"Where's my dog," Jack croaked.

"At the vet. He's okay. A couple of busted ribs and a big knot on his head. He'll be alright."

"I landed on him when we came to a stop. That must have broke his ribs," Jack explained. He was unable to talk and think with clarity. The deep dull pain behind his eyes was nauseating. Slight movement of the head hurt like hell.

"You've got a nasty concussion and a pretty big goose egg yourself. You rest. I just stopped to see how you're doing." A nurse whisked into the room and shooed him away.

"Talk to you later, Bub," Red said as he walked out the door.

By the next day Jack felt good enough to sit up. Sheriff Slade returned to talk to Jack about the accident. "Howdy Bub," he greeted Jack in his usual way. "You're looking better all the time. I actually think you just might make it." Red shook his friend's hand. "I thought retirement was supposed to be peaceful, kind of quiet," Red teased. His sincere grin gave the big man a slightly clownish look which when combined with the LBJ sized ears gave him a friendly hang dog look.

"Me too. Guess we were both wrong."

The two veteran cops talked about the accident and confirmed that it was Howland's Caddy that ran Jack off the road. Red filled Jack in on the beating of Sally and the subsequent car chase. Sally was in ICU with a severe concussion, broken face, and a heightened sense of victimization. Howland had completely disappeared in spite of the fact that everyone knew Doyle on sight. He was hard to miss with those two hooks and his obnoxious personality. Doyle had gone to ground, sliding into the dark side.

The cops were puzzled by how Doyle had gotten away. Even with squads on his tail and others setting up a road block ahead of him, he had disappeared. Jack chuckled when he heard his old friend express his frustration over Howland's escape.

"Go to the back of the cemetery. There's a trail that leads across the ridge and works its way down to that old field road along the creek. You know which road I'm talking about," Jack asked. Red nodded his affirmation. "I bet he ran into the cemetery and took that road. I'd check it out if I was you," Jack said. Indeed, they found parts of Doyle's car on the trail. Howland barked a few trees and left behind strips of chrome, headlight pieces, and pale yellow paint chips.

Before Doyle crossed paths with Jack he ran a teenager into a ditch, caused a drunk hitchhiker to fill his pants, and ran over two very nice people. Then when Jack figured he had heard the worst, Red told him about Father Dan and Cindy.

It made Jack sick to hear that Cindy lay down the hall with a broken leg and a broken heart. In an attempt to elude the cops, Howland had turned into the St. Mary's parking lot. With his headlights off, Doyle came around the corner of the church and ran smack dab into Cindy and Father Dan. As Jack had earlier suspected, Cindy had given her inebriated brother a ride home. She was helping Father Dan from the car to the house when Doyle hit Cindy and ran the priest over. The good Father took his last bloody gasping breath in the gravel drive of St. Mary's church. Doyle never slowed down.

Everyone in Brunswick knew that Jack Delaney had saved Doyle's life when he pulled him from the house fire many years before. Half of the cops on the Sheriff's Department thought Jack had done the right thing by saving Doyle's miserable life, because it was his duty. The other half were convinced that it had been a huge mistake. Red Slade decided to give Jack Delaney a second chance at Doyle Howland.

"I thought you'd like to help find the son of a bitch," Red said to his old friend.

"You bet your ass. You bet your ass," Jack quietly repeated with tears of determination running down his cheeks.

It wasn't long before Jack was on his feet and was sworn in again as a deputy. Father Dan was buried with great fanfare and profound sadness. Cindy had the church filled with flowers.

# CHAPTER TWENTY EIGHT

Father Dan was buried with full police honors. For thirty years he had been Father confessor, big brother, and chaplain to the Brunswick Sheriff's Department. If ever there was a friend to law enforcement, it was Father Daniel Robertson. Jack had known the man all of his life.

The honor guard consisted of six respected officers chosen by the Sheriff from the ranks of the department. A concussion, no matter how severe, was not about to keep Jack Delaney from performing his duty on the squad in honor of his friend.

One by one the six officers gathered in the basement of St. Mary's Catholic Church to get ready for the funeral. Their two-toned brown uniforms were cleaned, starched, and pressed. Bloused pants set off spit shined boots. All Smokey the Bear hats were squarely seated over determined faces.

Monsignor Murphy from the Diocese of LaCrosse had been asked by the family to conduct the mass. He and Father Dan had gone to seminary together in Rome and had been friends for all of their priestly lives. The Monsignor's political ambition and ability

landed him in his current position. Father Dan had never har-
bored such ambition. Often after numerous libations, Father Dan
would remark that he had no patience for the "political malarkey"
that went with moving up the ladder of the priesthood. He would
remind his good friend the Monsignor that "the farther up the
ladder you go the more your hind end shows." Rather, he wanted
simply "to tend to me flock."

Jack's turn at the casket came just as the mass of people
began filing through the vestibule. Jack stood at parade rest,
feet set shoulder width apart, hands clasped behind his back,
chin up, jaw set, looking straight past the shuffling, sniffling
crowd out through the open double doors into the sky beyond.
In silent honor to his friend, Jack studiously ignored all comments and questions as he paid a sentinel's tribute to his fallen
brother. All of his thoughts were focused on standing guard. It
took every ounce of available emotional will power to keep his
tears in check.

Years before Jack became a cop and Father Dan became a
priest, they had served together in the Wisconsin National Guard.
The day Richard Nixon resigned from office on August 9, 1974,
the two of them stood their posts for twelve hours. As with all
militia, their sworn allegiance was to the Constitution and its protection, not to the man. So on that day they stood their posts to
protect the Constitution as power was passed, peacefully if fitfully,
under its banner. They listened to a small transistor radio of the
proceedings as Richard Nixon resigned and Gerald Ford took the
oath of office. The two young men shared their respective dreams
about the choices and paths before them that day. Father Dan
heard the call to heal while Jack heard the call to protect. Both
answered their respective calls and marched in time to the drum
beat of their own heart.

Jack heard the Monsignor's eulogy from his post at the back
of the packed little church. He heard the sniffles and stifled sobs

from those in the church and from the crowd gathered outside on the steps and parking lot.

"It was grace that defined Father Dan," the Monsignor managed to choke out before losing control of his tears. He bowed his head and gripped the sides of the podium with his outstretched hands as he wept. The good priest shuddered, inhaled deeply, and shook his head as if willing himself to continue. When at last his composure held, he went on.

"Grace, Father Dan liked to say, is the only true evidence of God's presence in our lives. He would gently remind us all that love was easy compared to grace. Love usually begets love whereas grace has no expectation of reward. That was Father Dan's conclusion after ministering to his flock for 30 years. We are all aware of his weekly reminder that 'A little grace goes a long ways.' " Warming to his subject, Monsignor Murphy gave the sermon of his life. While Jack agreed with everything the priest said, he remembered little of it. Everything blurred into a hum until Herb Robertson sang Amazing Grace in honor of his brother. After burial, Taps, and church lunch, Jack left exhausted.

His exhaustion drove him towards home, but restlessness caused him to turn into the driveway of the Graves farm. Fall had brought golden days. A persistent yellowing of the fall foliage turned positively brilliant with the setting of the sun. Shadows danced against the house as a soft wind played in the oaks. He was sure Anna wouldn't mind if he took the old tractor out for a stroll. As the tractor splashed across the creek and growled up through the woods, Jack thought about the death of Father Dan. He blamed himself for Cindy's injuries and Father Dan's death. If he had let that son of a bitch Howland die in the fire all those years ago, none of this would have happened. Nothing good had ever come from saving the man's life. Nothing. He was a burr in every saddle of everyone he had ever come across. And now the son of a bitch had killed a very good man. It made Jack sick.

He parked the tractor in the shade of a big oak tree. The fall air was cool and dry. Closing his eyes, Jack leaned his head back against the oak tree resting in the shade. A faint whisper of breeze rustled the tall grass as the setting sun brought out its golden hue. Somewhere between his tears and dusk, Jack fell asleep. Awakened to the sound of crickets, he listened to their chirping in the fading light. It was the only sound except for the slight stirring of the leaves. A crescent moon framed the big oak and low wispy clouds reflected the pinkish light of sunset. Stiff from lying on the ground and emotionally spent from crying, Jack got to his feet and stretched.

The metal fender of the tractor was cool to the touch as he grabbed it for a hand hold to get up onto the seat. The starter ground a few times before the engine caught and sputtered to life. He feathered the choke and adjusted the throttle until it ran smooth. Then he made his slow way back through the darkened woods to the shed. Although life had never felt so empty, he knew what he had to do. It was time to bring Doyle Howland to justice. But first he needed a new pair of boots.

# CHAPTER TWENTY NINE

Behind every good detective is a great source. Molly McIntyre was the best source Jack Delaney ever had. She was a peddler in the old school sense in that she bought and sold just about everything. At Molly's Mercantile you could buy guns, jewelry, old records, new western boots, coins and clothes. A cluttered shabbiness permeated the place. At one time or another, just about every resident of Brunswick came through her door. She had a keen ear for gossip and a fine eye for B.S. Although it was rare that she passed on information, when she did it was gold.

Molly had liked Jack ever since he gave her kid a break years before. It had been a small thing to give the kid a talking to instead of an arrest record, and Molly had appreciated the gesture.

Over the years, Jack had purchased several pairs of boots from Molly. He never came in asking for information, nor did she give him information in return for buying a pair of boots. More often than not she told him nothing. But once in a while Molly would come through. Since Jack knew that she and Sally were friends, it was just possible that she might have something to offer.

As he tried on this pair of boots and that, they talked about Father Dan and the man who had killed him. Molly inquired about Cindy and the bar. Jack brought her up to date on what he knew. Although she seemed interested, he was quite sure that Molly had as much information about the case as he did.

As he paid for yet another pair of boots, Molly casually mentioned that she had been to visit Sally at the nursing home where she was attempting to recover from her brutal beating. With disgust, Molly commented that during one of Sally's lapses of consciousness during Doyle's rampage, she awoke with him standing over her urinating in her face. The incident had been documented in the police report. Molly suggested that maybe Jack should pay Sally a visit. Jack thanked Molly and drove to the nursing home. He realized that a message had been passed that Sally was willing to cooperate with Jack.

The harassed desk clerk directed Jack to a room at the end of the hall. The nauseating ammonia smell from urine soaked clothes was barely disguised by the disinfectant. Jack swore he'd step in front of a train before someone would put him in a place like this for the remainder of his days. He negotiated the long hall as one might an obstacle course. Rotting, dying, drooling residents shuffled, wheeled, or sat along this hallway of hell. Burdened staff, undone and overwhelmed by the work, misery, and suffering, scurried about performing their endless thankless tasks.

Doyle Howland's last official act in his relationship with Sally was to give her one last boot to the face before stomping out of her apartment door. The damage to her optical nerve left her stone blind. Before this final indignity hoisted upon her by Doyle Howland, Sally had not been the policeman's friend. For whatever reason, she had lied and covered for Doyle Howland for many years. Jack was constantly amazed at how much abuse a person would take before they finally turned on their attackers and abusers. Sally had apparently reached her limit. During the surgery to repair damage to her crushed and broken scull, Sally had suffered a stroke that left her partially paralyzed. Blind and unable to move her left side, there was nowhere else for her to turn but the county home. It was the place of last abandonment.

Jack did not ask her any questions. He simply talked to her. The trouble with most detectives is that they get their pad and pen out too soon. They want to get the facts recorded before they are lost to time. And to be fair, most detectives are overworked with more cases than they can handle so it is natural for them to get right down to business. However, Jack Delaney was no ordinary detective.

He almost always interviewed or talked to witnesses two or three times. He rarely pressured them for information that they may or may not be willing to part with to a policeman. He never lied to them and respected their particular situation. In the end, he solved more cases than anyone on the Sheriff's Department in his quiet respectful way. On this visit to the nursing home, Jack never mentioned Doyle Howland. He only talked to Sally about her predicament. Her main concern was her mother who depended on Sally as her only source of care. Jack promised to look in on her.

After his first visit, Jack left her alone for a week. In the meantime he stopped to see Sally's elderly mother. He gave his card and told her to call him if she needed anything. Additionally, he changed a light bulb over the kitchen sink, set a mouse trap, and took her to the grocery store. When he next saw Sally, her gratitude was obvious.

Sally then confessed to Jack that she was deathly afraid of Doyle Howland. "He'll kill me the next time he sees me," she said quietly in the gathering darkness of the room. It was late in the day and no lights had been turned on in the room for Sally. Jack took Sally's hand.

"Sally, this is my only case. I will stay on it until Doyle Howland is either in jail or dead. That's my promise to you." Sally was silent for a long time. He wiped the tears rolling down her cheeks and then took her hand again. For a while they sat quietly in the gathering darkness.

"Duluth. That's the only place I can think that he would go. There's a guy there. His name is Slim. That's all I know. Whenever he got into real trouble, he called Slim."

Once outside of the nursing home he breathed deeply of the fresh air and tried to get the putrid smell of the place out of his nostrils. He couldn't so he took out his small jar of Vicks and put a little bit in each nostril. It was an old cop's trick used at death scenes to mask rotting bodies.

Back in town he stopped at the Brunswick Café to take care of some additional business. As he had been working the county for information, he had noticed Herb's car showing up at odd times and places as if he was following Jack. When he saw Herb's car parked at the Brunswick Café he decided to stop in for a visit. Herb was sitting in a booth sipping on coffee and nibbling on a piece of toast. Herb didn't eat very much. It got in the way of his drinking.

"Mind if I sit down," Jack indicated towards the empty side of the booth and sat down with his coffee when Herb nodded to do so. They talked about the weather and how things were changing around town. They talked about Cindy and Father Dan. Herb asked about Sally.

Jack finally got around to his purpose. He mentioned that he'd run across Herb's car quite a few times while out investigating the death of his brother, Father Dan. He told him that it almost seemed as if Herb was following him around. Herb said nothing. Jack mentioned that some people might think Herb was trying to find Doyle himself.

"If by chance you run across him, you'll let me know won't you," Jack asked.

Herb just looked at him. Jack neither warned Herb to stay out of the investigation, nor did he caution him not to take the law into his own hands. First of all, he knew it would do no good. Second, he was not all together sure he had the right to make such a request. Jack wanted him to know that he was aware of what Herb was up to. Herb could act upon that information as he pleased. With that understanding, Jack finished his coffee and left. He made his daily round to check on Cindy and then dropped off his dog. It was time to go to Duluth.

# CHAPTER THIRTY

J ack left for Duluth before Anna got back to the farm. She had sent him a letter before she left Arizona, telling him that she was pregnant. But when she got home, she found a note on the table which said,

> "I figured I better leave you a note just in case you got back before me. I'm in Duluth looking for Doyle Howland. He killed Father Dan and hurt Cindy with his car. I intend to bring him in. I left you some newspapers so that you can read up on the whole thing. Jack."

There was nothing in the note to reveal whether Jack had received or read the letter from Anna. She read the newspaper articles and then drove to the Brunswick Café to talk to Bud. Over coffee they caught up on all of the local news and about Anna's pregnancy.

"Jack is sure going to be surprised," Bud offered.

"I sent him a letter just before I left. I told him he is going to be a father. Maybe he knows," Anna replied.

"Hard to say."

The object of Anna's thoughts was sitting on a rock at the artesian well in Washburn. Jack sipped water and basked in the waning light of a magnificent fall day. There were no campers this time of year so the green expanse was uninterrupted by tents and pop-ups. The waters of Lake Superior were calm and the air was cool.

Autumn was further advanced up north than it was 150 miles south where Jack lived. The brilliant reds and oranges had faded or fallen. All that was left were yellows and rusts. The low level wispy clouds filtered an already weakening sun. Its light diffused and power to warm diminished as the Earth shifted towards its winter axis.

Jack just didn't know what to make of things. His jumbled motives for tracking Doyle left him feeling unsettled. It was personal to him on more than one level. Howland had killed a very good friend. For that, he wanted to kill the son of a bitch. Then there was his guilt over saving Doyle's life in the first place. He berated himself for the thousandth time. If only he had let Doyle burn himself up all those years ago, none of this would have happened. On top of everything else, Cindy had been hurt once again because of Howland. He was goddamn sure there would be no gratuitous life saving efforts this time around.

Then, of course, there was the pain in his heart for Anna. He had no idea where that relationship was headed or if Anna was coming home again. But for now he had a job to do in Duluth.

Leaving Washburn at dawn, Jack took County Road C North to Cornucopia. He grabbed a cup of coffee to go then took Highway 13 across the northern tip of Wisconsin to Duluth. Along the way he stopped and listened as Lake Superior splashed against the rocks. Two full grown bald eagles circled silently over the mouth of the Iron River where it dumped into the lake. He was glad for his leather jacket. The wind off the lake was sharp.

When he arrived at the Duluth police department, he asked for Detective Lewis. Before leaving Brunswick, Jack had made contact with the Duluth detective and explained the purpose of the trip up north. Lewis had said for him to come on up.

He liked Detective John Lewis immediately. A warm handshake, a welcoming manner, and a sense of humor greeted Jack Delaney. He judged Lewis to be about his own age. It appeared that numerous donuts during work and plenty of beer afterwards had combined with a lack of exercise to give Lewis some girth. Balding and red complected, Lewis had a ready smile and a twinkle in his eye.

"I was just about to go outside for a smoke. Mind talking outside," not waiting for the answer Lewis headed for the door. "I feel like a goddamn criminal around here. Got to sneak outside to smoke for Christ's sake." As Lewis led Jack towards the door, he heard groans and comments from the other detectives. Someone grumbled for Lewis to shut up. Once outside the door, Lewis lit up a cigarette. Blowing the smoke away from Jack, he said "they're just jealous because I'm so damn good looking. So, you're looking for Slim, huh?"

"Sure am," Jack replied.

"He's hard to miss. If there's something bad going on in Duluth, Slim is somewhere around. Only trouble is, he's smart enough not to get caught," Lewis explained. Rubbing his belly, Lewis shifted gears from Slim to the thought of food without skipping a beat. "I'm hungry as shit, let's eat." With that, they headed for the parking lot and Lewis' unmarked squad.

At the restaurant, which was dominated by cops, they found a place at the counter. After ordering a couple of specials, they got down to business talking about Slim. The place was noisy with lively conversations creating a buzz louder than the sum of its parts, which in turn provided coverage for individual conversations.

"We've never been able to catch him at anything big. He's gotten some slaps for small things, but he's gotten away with the big stuff. Basically, Slim's a facilitator. If you need something, he's the guy to go to. However, he's rarely at the scene of the crime," Lewis explained as he dove into his food. As he devoured the hot beef sandwich with mashed potatoes and gravy, Lewis managed to fill in the gaps about Slim. "And no one rats him out. He's too valuable to his friends and he kills his enemies. Slim is one bad dude. Basically, Slim's the smallest, smartest, meanest, redneck bastard you'll ever meet. After lunch we'll look around."

They drove around, talking to various sources, looking for Slim. They went to Slim's place of business, a chop shop, and to his shit hole of a house, but they did not find Slim nor did they find anyone willing to say where he had gone. At the chop shop the guys wouldn't talk or let them look around. The place was ostensibly a machine shop, but everyone knew its real purpose. Slim's house was surrounded by a six foot high chain link fence and it was patrolled by two very mean looking Rottweilers.

Lewis was an authority on nearly every subject. However, no matter what the subject was it always looped back to the topic of women. It appeared that women were Lewis' great study in life. "Yeah, he's a slippery son of a bitch. I suppose that's why we haven't caught him. Christ! Look at that ass, will ya," pointing to a shapely young professional walking across the street in front of the squad car.

Jack was not surprised to learn that Lewis had been married numerous times. At present, he was married to a young bartender that he had become involved with while married to his second wife. Wife number three was home taking care of the baby. Lewis explained that he had a number of children from his previous two marriages. He was paying child support for some of those kids, alimony to one of his ex wives, and now he had to support a new wife and child. That was the reason why he was still working and not retired. Lewis described his own situation as "not being able to keep my rocket in my pocket." He laughed, adding, "I guess it's the fuckin' I get for the fuckin' I got."

By the end of the day, Lewis and Jack had been to enough chop shops, pawn shops, dives, seedy apartments, and places of disrepute to last a lifetime. Lewis traversed the seedy landscape with ease. At times he joked around, at others he threatened. In some instances, Lewis was the understanding ear. Then he played the bad cop ready to do anything inside or outside of the law to get the cooperation that he sought. All with no success.

Jack picked up his truck at the station and went back to his hotel room for a shower and a nap. The truck had been repaired from the accident and was once again in excellent condition. He promised Lewis that he would meet him later at a cops' bar that was pointed out to him by Lewis earlier in the day.

By the time Jack reached the Badge-and-Brief a major party was underway. Apparently, Thursday nights were big at the B&B. Lawyers, secretaries, and courthouse staff rubbed elbows with each other and with the ever present cops. Jack figured that like most cops' bars, they rubbed more than elbows.

Jack was barely inside the door when he was flagged down by Lewis' gesturing from the middle of the bar. He wedged, shouldered, and excused himself through a crowd which was extremely engaged with itself. When he finally made it to Lewis he found himself included in a tight circle of people well on their way towards inebriation. At bar closing time they went to the apartment of one of the female cops. There a bunch of them partied until dawn. Jack fell asleep on the couch. He roused himself and went back to his hotel room for some additional sleep. Somewhere in mid-morning the phone rang and it was Lewis.

"Delaney," he shouted into the receiver. "Our boy called. Left a message. Get your ass down here pronto," hanging up.

At the station Lewis played him Slim's message,

"Lewis. This is Slim. Heard you dudes were looking for me. Sorry I missed you. Heh, heh. The boys said you were asking about Doyle. He was here a while ago. Stayed a few days but took off. Not sure where he went man, but he's got friends in Illinois. He left his car in my garage. It's all yours if you want it. Gotta go, man. I'll be back in a few weeks. Give me a call if you need anything else. Don't worry none 'bout the dogs."

Slim delivered enough goods on Howland to get the cops off his back for a little bit, while offering Howland some limited protection. Truth be known, Doyle had never been a favorite of Slim's. More trouble than he was worth. So if the cops got him, all the better.

"See what I mean," Lewis asked. "He's goddamn clever. He gives up Howland without giving up anything else and covers his own ass."

They went to Slim's house and found the gate open, the dogs gone, and the garage unlocked. Inside Jack saw Howland's rusted Caddy through a grimy window. Lewis wanted to go straight into the garage, but Jack stopped him. He explained the necessity of doing this one by the book and Lewis reluctantly went along with Jack's request.

Upon securing the warrant, they did a cursory search of the car. It appeared that it had been in the garage for some time. Jack made arrangements for the removal of the Cadillac and its transport back to the Brunswick Sheriff's Department. Jack bid Lewis farewell, then escorted the Caddy back home. Once it was impounded, he went to get his dog.

# CHAPTER THIRTY ONE

O n the way to pick up Harry, Jack pulled on his headlights even though it was mid-afternoon. Heavy fog clung to the earth. It was like driving through a white painting where all of the figures are simply shades of the same colorless landscape. Here and there were splashes of color. A red barn or a yellow caution sign looming out of the gloom, fighting for individuality in the enveloping gray mist, making Jack blue.

When Cindy learned of Jack's Duluth trip, she insisted that Harry be left in her care. Her recovery was slow. Outfitted with a walking cast and cane, Cindy navigated her apartment with difficulty. But she insisted that Harry would pose no problem and the company would do her good.

During Cindy's recovery, Jack had appointed himself as her chief care giver and protector. He took her to see the doctor, grocery shopped for her, cooked and cleaned her apartment. The one thing he did not volunteer to do was operate the tavern, which stayed closed during her recovery.

Cindy greeted him from her spot on the couch surrounded by pillows, pills, and other accouterments of a recovering patient, all within easy reach. Her partially cast leg was propped up to take pressure off healing bones. The reading lamp basked Cindy in its soft, warm glow.

After settling Harry down to an acceptable level and greeting Cindy, Jack took out the trash. He pocketed the grocery list she had prepared, grabbed a beer, and sat down opposite Cindy in the easy chair. They caught up on his trip to Duluth. He spared no details describing the events of the investigation. Cindy possessed an intense desire to see Doyle Howland behind bars. Harry sat at Jack's feet pawing at Jack's leg whenever the attention flagged. Finally, Jack put him in a down position and rubbed his ears. As he talked with Cindy he noticed that she seemed preoccupied.

"Everything okay," he asked. She nodded in a tentative way and looked into her lap. Jack had seen that look many times.

"Alright, what's up," he leaned forward and scooted to the edge of the chair as he prodded her. Cindy began crying and refused to look up at Jack or answer him. He moved to her side and took her hand.

"Come on now. What's the matter?"

"Oh Jack," she sobbed and leaned into him as he put his arm around her shoulders. He let her cry it out and held her until she recovered. "It's Anna. She's back."

Jack said nothing. He honestly did not know what to say and it was the last thing he expected to hear. Cindy ventured a sideways glance at him to gauge his response. "The color is gone from your face," Cindy said softly.

"I'm sorry Cindy. You know I don't mean to hurt you," Jack said.

Cindy had carried a slim hope that Anna would not return. Now that hope was crushed. For a while the two of them just sat together holding hands, exhausted by their emotional labors. Neither said anything. Cindy dabbed her eyes a time or two. The lump in Jack's throat kept him between tears and silence.

"Can I ask you a question," Cindy broke the silence.

"Sure."

"You really care for her, don't you?"

"Yes," he said after a long pause.

"God that hurts," Cindy again lapsed into tears. They stayed where they were until the light of the day faded to darkness. Harry was asleep at their feet. Cindy shut off the light and pulled Jack to her. She whispered to him that Anna would have him for the rest of his life; she only wanted to hold him for a little while longer.

Cindy had learned about the baby from the ever present Brunswick gossip mill. Debating all day whether to tell him, she finally decided Anna should be the one to tell him. And for sure as she was alive, Cindy knew Jack would leave her bed and go straight to Anna. While it broke her heart, she knew where his love resided and it was not with her. She had resigned herself to the fact that he had already gone to Anna deep in his heart and he was not coming back to her.

"Have you told her that you love her," Cindy asked. Hesitating, Jack finally stammered "I'm sure I have." Jack searched his memory, but wasn't sure if he had.

"You and I have been together off and on for forty years. How many times have you told me that you love me? Few and far between, I'll tell you that," Cindy said with an edge. "Well, God dammit Jack, you better make sure you tell her." A head of steam was building.

"I'm sorry," was all he could manage.

"Go to her now Jack. Go now. Tell her you love her. Make a commitment for Christ's sakes. I've had enough Jack. I've waited forty years and I've lost. Go to her," Cindy turned and cried into her pillow as she curled up into a ball for emotional protection. "Please go," she whispered. Jack didn't quite know what to do as usual, but did as he was bidden. He gathered up his things and collected Harry. The last thing he did before leaving was to put the grocery list back under the refrigerator magnet. Closing the door quietly behind him he believed that he was leaving Cindy for the last time.

The headlights of Old Blue barely penetrated the fog as he sat in the parking lot facing Stoney Lonesome Road. His internal fog left him confused and uncertain. Sick at heart over Cindy and scared to death about Anna, Jack sat with the engine idling for several minutes.

Wiping tears of sadness and anticipation from his cheeks, he was surprised to find himself crying. Caught between his past and his future, he found reluctance in leaving and anxiety in going. In the end, he drove home. Jack decided to drop Harry at the house, check his mail, clean up, and then call Anna; but he found himself suddenly exhausted.

Jack controlled a near uncontrollable urge to call Anna the moment he walked into the house. But the lateness of the hour fueled his natural good sense and he showered instead. He had all he could do to towel off and flop on the bed. His mail sat in an unopened pile on his kitchen counter. Harry waited for Jack to fall asleep and then snuck up on the bed. Jack snored softly and made no movement as Harry settled down next to him.

Sometime in mid-morning Jack crawled from bed and brewed his coffee. Absently, Jack flipped through the mail as he sipped his coffee. His heart nearly stopped and he almost dropped his coffee cup when he found the letter from Anna.

Upon reading the words "baby" Jack left coffee, mail, and dog behind as he rushed to the farm. He could not have known that Cindy watched him round the corner by the tavern and accelerate out of sight as he hurried down Stoney Lonesome Road. There was also no way for him to know that while one woman disintegrated into tears, another wondered if he'd show up at all.

Anna had been waiting to hear from Jack since she got back to the farm. When pacing failed to provide the necessary vent to her pent up emotions, she went for long walks on the farm. While the exercise was a healthy way to burn steam, the anxiety could not be tamed. Anna drove by his house so many times it made her feel like a stalker.

It didn't help that the weather had been the picture of gloom. She was finding it hard to adjust to the lack of sun which had failed to shine since her return to the farm. As she curled her naked body into her quilt, Anna felt her growing belly and dreamed about her baby. At the very least her problem about the alcove was solved. It was the perfect nursery.

As she floated in the ether of dream sleep, a distinct familiar distant sound pulled at the edge of her consciousness. Anna returned to consciousness just as Jack turned into the driveway. The sound that had been clawing at her was Old Blue's distinctive growl. Flying from her bed she glimpsed the truck through her window, grabbed her robe, and raced for the stairway.

They met in the kitchen amidst tears, apologies, and expressions of undying love. All gloom disappeared and the heaviness in their hearts evaporated. Jack dropped to his knees and wrapped his arms around her middle while laying his head on her belly. Anna held his head and stroked his hair. Tears of relief broke forth freeing the pain in their hearts, releasing an indescribable joy.

Sir Isaac Newton said that for every action there is a reaction. Every positive electric charge carries with it a negative one. For every yin there is a yang. Up Stoney Lonesome Road a few miles, this mirrored phenomenon played itself out. Crushed, Cindy lay motionless under a leaden blanket of grief.

# CHAPTER THIRTY TWO

R esettling at the farm, Jack completed the nursery. As he pounded, plastered, and painted the alcove, it gratified Jack that his carpentry skills were finally being put to worthy use. Nothing in his life had given him greater satisfaction than making a home for his little girl. An amniocentesis test had confirmed the news that a healthy baby girl was on the way.

"Mattie Anne Delaney" was sewn, embroidered, and stenciled throughout the alcove. The old writing space was now Mattie Anne's Room. Soft shades of pink frosted with delicate white lace gave the pretty little space a fairy tale look. All winter long they worked on Mattie Anne's space. Anna poured herself into making everything just right.

But with much on his mind, Jack took a well earned break from his family duties to go off and think. The trail at the back of the Brunswick cemetery, the one that Howland took to escape, wound along the ridge and went around a high rocky knob. From his perch upon this highest point in Brunswick County, Jack could view his past, present, and future with a sweep of the eye. Bundled against the cold air, he sat watching the pale, setting winter sun redden the horizon. In one direction he could see the lights of the City of Brunswick. In another he could see Stoney Lonesome Road wind through the landscape, past the Robertson, Howland, and Graves farms. In the distance he glimpsed Hank's Place.

The perch was known as Elk Mound. For hundreds of years the indigenous people used this vantage point to spot herds of elk. The lookout still provided an unmatched eagles' view of the world Jack loved. His whole life had been lived within the limit of his vision. It was while watching the world below that Jack decided to let the murder of Sonny Howland go. He concluded that it was unsolvable even with the tantalizing glimmers that came from the letters and poems. "I've got more important things to do now," Jack said out loud to the sky as he thought of his little family below. His impending fatherhood made him feel whole like nothing else in the world had ever done.

But before he could rest, Doyle Howland had to be brought to justice. Brought in or killed. Either way would suit Jack Delaney just fine. Jack had a notion that when confronted, Doyle would play his hand to the end. The only real surprise for Jack was the arson materials found in the car. Gas cans, a timer, ignition devices, and rags were laid out in the caddy's trunk. The target was unknown, but it gave Jack a queasy feeling. It made the hair on the back of his neck stand up. Why did this fact make him so uneasy? He decided to go to work the next day and make a last stab at bringing in the bad guy.

The next morning, Anna asked to tag along for the day. At the Sheriff's Department, Jack and Anna reviewed the reports and photos. They walked the crime scene at the church, then drove to Doyle's trailer where they let themselves inside. "God, it smells in here," Anna complained as the stale, sour air rushed to get out as they opened the door. All the lights turned on could not erase the gloom so Jack turned on his kel light. "What are we looking for," she asked. "Don't know for sure. But the place sort of haunts me. I've been in here a half a dozen times and get the willies every time I step foot inside," he admitted.

Anna walked around in the dingy smelly place gingerly so as not to touch a thing. She picked her way to the back bedroom where she found Jack staring into an open closet. Without turning around, Jack asked "why do I keep coming back to this room." He then turned to Anna who was standing in the doorway. Continuing, Jack explained, "Whenever I am in this trailer, I am drawn to this room. Don't know why. Just a feeling." Anna remained in the doorway.

Her stomach had started to turn even before she caught her image in the tiny mirror lying on the dresser by the door. It was the last thing she remembered before fainting. With Jack's assistance, she got to her feet. As Anna looked at the mirror again she threw up all over Jack.

"I think we better get you out of here." As Jack began to guide her down the hall towards the front door, Anna grabbed the mirror. Once outside, she gulped the fresh air.

"Oh my God, I never ...want to...to...go in there...again," she gasped. "This is my mirror. How did he get my mirror?"

The mirror had been given to her as a present from her mother. Its silver handle, polished smooth from years of use, now had scratch marks made by a man with hooks for hands. It was now obvious that Doyle Howland had been in their house. The little mirror had been missing for quite a while.

Doyle Howland's presence at the farm could have only one explanation, he meant them harm. Certainly Howland did not burgle their house to take a small mirror. The only conclusion was the intended ill will of Doyle Howland against them. It made even more sense in light of the gas cans found in Doyle's trunk. Jack concluded that these facts had to be related.

"The son of a bitch must have grabbed the mirror when he was casing the house," he stated. Anna agreed, although the thought of Doyle's presence in her home was revolting. "Why would he be in our house? What does he want with us," she asked while trying hard to quell a rising panic.

Although Jack momentarily thought of protecting Anna from the information about the gas cans, he decided she had a right to know. So he told her that Doyle must have intended to burn down their house.

"All I can think of is that he is trying to settle an old score between his family and yours. It's all that makes sense," Jack explained.

Jack went back onto the Doyle Howland case with a vengeance. He reasoned that Howland must have watched them in order to ascertain their habits. The only place to do that was from the cemetery above the farm. Jack found Pall Mall cigarette butts and empty beer cans in the far corner at the back of the cemetery. Damn, Jack said to himself, the bastard has been watching us.

It was time to go back and visit Sally.

# CHAPTER THIRTY THREE

Jack was warmly received when he stopped in to see Sally at the nursing home. She brightened at the sound of his voice. Sally was strapped in her chair listening to the drone of a soap opera re-run playing on the T.V. Visitors were infrequent and the T.V. was her only break from the monotony of paralysis and the pain of despair. In her good hand she clutched a rosary.

"Doing okay," he asked, taking her hand.

"Okay I guess. Some feeling is coming back in my leg. They say with therapy I might get some use back."

"Have the ladies from the church been around to see you?"

"Yes. Besides you they are the only visitors I get. Mom can't get here by herself and they sometimes bring her. Thank you so much."

"They do a nice job."

"Yes, they do," she agreed.

"Sally, I'm sorry to ask you again about Doyle. But I have to. We found some gas cans in his car. It looked like he was going to start something on fire. Does that sound familiar to you at all," Jack asked.

"When I saw the gas cans he told me to forget about it. That they were for someone very special."

"Did he say who?"

"No. But he was always talking about getting even with the Graves. He hated them so bad," she said and pausing with a frown for a beat – she continued. "I remember a little. All he talked about the last couple weeks was how much he hated that girl, the granddaughter. I'm sorry I couldn't tell you all of this before," Sally apologized.

"That's all right. Don't worry about that at all. Just tell me what you remember. That's enough," Jack reassured her. "Doyle ever mention being out at the Graves farm?"

"Not that I remember."

Jack thanked her for her help and promised to check on her mother. As he drove home, Jack's determination to catch Doyle hardened. The information Sally provided fueled his determination, but nothing in her revelations brought Jack closer to catching him. It was standard police procedure, luck, and the vagaries of life that did that.

The phone call from the Springfield, Illinois Police Department was pure luck. The cops got lucky that Doyle Howland simply could not help but be himself. It was human folly that caused Doyle Howland to draw attention to himself and get the cops involved.

The APB on Howland had alerted the Illinois authorities. According to the detective from Springfield, Doyle had settled in with a local prostitute. Doyle had managed to elude a coordinated manhunt for months. No one had known of his whereabouts. Then his mean, nasty nature betrayed him. Once an asshole, always an asshole, Jack mused to himself. Howland had been discovered after he had assaulted a convenience store clerk. Doyle had gone to the convenience store late at night to get cigarettes. While there, he decided to put gas in the car.

Doyle was unable to put gas into the car because of his hooks and he had to ask the store attendant for help. He prepaid and went back to his car to wait. The kid behind the counter, Ralphie by the stitching on his shirt, had a customer to wait on before he could fill the tank. Because Doyle was impatient by nature and drunk by choice, he began to lay on the horn. The kid ignored him. Finally after a few more minutes of studied indifference, the attendant came to pump the gas.

"What took you so fucking long, Ralphie," Doyle snarled, but Ralphie ignored him and went about his business pumping gas into Doyle's tank. Doyle was not the first drunken asshole that Ralphie had had to deal with.

"I asked you a question you little prick."

Ralphie, the smarter of the two by far, continued to ignore Doyle's taunts. Smart as he was, Ralphie couldn't have known that the worst insult to Doyle Howland was to be ignored. In order to get Ralphie's attention, Doyle clawed at him with one of his hooks and scraped Ralphie's arm, finally getting his attention.

Ralphie jumped back and shouted "you bastard." Then he grabbed the nozzle and used it to beat back Doyle's attack. Doyle started the car and drove off, but not before Ralphie got a good look at the car. He also remembered that he had seen this car on numerous occasions being driven by a woman whom Ralphie was able to describe with some specificity. The police were able to track down the woman and identified her as a local prostitute. She must have been desperate to take Doyle Howland into her life. She told police that he was on the lamb from the cops and proud of it. He told her that they wanted him for murder so she had better mind her p's and q's. She complained that he had been a mean bastard and she was glad to get rid of him. So much for honor among thieves.

A description of the car and its license plate along with a description of the driver was put out immediately after Ralphie reported the incident to the police. Jack drove straight to Springfield upon learning that Howland was in the area. He joined a young detective for the search. Jack told the police, "Be careful," Jack warned him. "He'll run over anyone who gets in his way."

Doyle was flushed out of his lair on the north side of town. He was spotted crossing the street through an alley trying to elude the police. Within minutes the entire area was crawling with cops and three of them were able to box Doyle into a corner. Jack was in one of the squads. But before anyone could react, Doyle slammed his car into reverse and backed into Jack and the young detective. Because his seatbelt had been unlocked in anticipation of getting out of the car, the detective smacked the steering wheel with his head upon impact. Doyle rammed them again and moved the squad enough to slip by, once again eluding their grasp.

Jack slid the bleeding and unconscious cop to the side and got behind the wheel. Doyle's taillights were out and it was difficult to keep track of his location as they flew through the alley. Crossing street after street they were locked in the quintessential chase. One of the biggest adrenaline rushes that a cop will ever experience is the high speed chase. The bad guy has to run. The cop has to chase. It is a very human thing to do.

Jack Delaney chased Howland as if the world's survival depended upon it. His only illumination was the red bubble light on the roof of the car. The headlights of the squad had been smashed out when Doyle rammed them. Jack kept the siren at fever pitch.

Doyle screeched out onto a main street and then turned quickly down a side street. The short block ended at what appeared to be a gated park. Doyle never slowed down, smashing through the gates with Jack following along. Jack quickly realized that he was in a cemetery, not a park.

Doyle took a hard right and disappeared up over a hill. By the time Jack made the turn Doyle was coming back down the hill straight at him. Doyle had mistakenly turned into a dead-end parking lot. Jack swerved, but was struck in the right front of his car and was driven sideways and back into a tree. Doyle's car stopped in the middle of the road, running. The illumination from the red bubble light gave the rising radiator steam a Hades-like quality. Jack stepped into the street with his gun drawn and hammer cocked. His stainless steel Model 66 Smith and Wesson .357 glowed with each pulse of light.

For a heartbeat there was a standoff. Then Doyle floored it straight towards Jack who pulled the trigger on the big gun until the windshield was gone. At the last moment, Jack jumped to the side. The car veered off to the left and came to rest against a large headstone. Bursting into flames the car illuminated a monument on the hill behind Jack. It was only then that Jack realized he was at the base of Lincoln's tomb. Within moments, the cavalry arrived.

In the thirty-five years that Jack Delaney had been a policeman he had never fired his gun in the line of duty. Now the demanding hand of fate had required him to kill.

Although Jack was cleared of any wrongdoing, it was another thing to live with it. He saw to it that Doyle's remains were brought home and buried next to his parents in the Brunswick cemetery. The American Legion provided a plaque, a flag, and a military salute. The same honor they offered every deceased veteran.

Not one person came forward to claim the body or attend to its burial. Jack had always believed that if a man couldn't find six people to carry the remains, then that life hadn't been worth much. Doyle's death fostered no sympathy or loss. Herb Robertson had silently shook Jack's hand.

More than one person said, "It's about time."

# CHAPTER THIRTY FOUR

Anna relaxed in her last weeks of pregnancy. All her grand-mother's papers had now been thoroughly gone through. In their entirety, there was nothing new about the murder. Nor had any light been shed on the true identity of her grandfather. But that somehow seemed almost beside the point. The full and rich picture of her grandmother's life had come into focus in spite of the missing puzzle pieces. She had filled several notebooks with the life of Mattie Beret Graves. Mattie's own words, in the form of prose and poem, graced the handwritten pages of an adoring granddaughter's journal. Anna's love and respect for her grand-mother grew in proportion to the time spent sifting through the pages of her life.

The Robert Frost thesis was not going to be finished in this life-time. Anna abandoned the master's degree, having had enough of the university. By mutual agreement, they went their separate ways. Instead, she focused on the life of her grandmother. Anna had filled her journals with her thoughts about her grandmother's life and memories and experiences that she had shared with her. For hours at a time Anna sat in the alcove and worked on the story of Mattie Beret Graves. Whenever Anna rocked and read from the journal, Mattie Anne was calm.

Pausing momentarily from her reading, Anna listened to the rain through the open window. Relaxing back into the rocking chair, she closed her eyes and rested her hands on her belly. A cool breeze carried the fresh scent of an early spring rain.

Harry lay across the open doorway. The big dog spent increasing amounts of time by her side. On occasion, he would lay his head in her lap and look up at her with those big, gentle eyes.

Ever since Jack had returned from Springfield he had been quieter than usual. All he said when he got home was that it was over. Anna noticed that Jack locked his service revolver away and did not take it back out again. She would often find him on the porch, rocking away the long hours before dawn.

Anna's daydream was interrupted as Jack stuck his head in the door. "Hi. Whatcha doin," he asked. Anna just smiled and lifted her journal off her lap, holding it up in explanation. Jack came over and gave Anna a kiss on the forehead. "I see you've been reading to Mattie again," he said. She took his hand and held it against her cheek.

"I like sitting here with Mattie Anne. I picture her everywhere in this room," Anna said as she freed his hand. He absentmindedly leaned down and looked out the open window into the yard below.

"I've been giving some thought to finishing up the widow's estate. I still have to take that picture to the lady in the Cities. Maybe this would be a good time to do that. What do you think," he asked while remaining at the window.

Anna preferred to have him with her every minute in the last moments of her pregnancy. But she realized that Jack was restless and probably needed something to get his mind off the heavy burden of having killed a man. She of course gave him her blessing, but extracted a promise that he come right home.

Rebecca Fitzgerald's Will had been explicit that her favorite picture of her husband be delivered to her first cousin Winifred

"Tippy" Gamble of St. Clair Street, St. Paul, Minnesota. It was the same picture that Jack had retrieved for the widow as she lay dying in the hospital.

The delivery was a simple matter of driving over to the Twin Cities some afternoon. Following up on the information provided by the probate lawyer, Jack set up an appointment. Within a few days he was on his way to St. Paul.

St. Clair Avenue is near Summit Avenue and plays host to block after block of graceful and stately homes. It is the neighborhood of Victoria's Crossing with its uptown shops and coffee houses. Just down the block is The Lexington, a venerated restaurant frequented by the heavyweights of the community. Up a block is the Law School. A tough no nonsense practical legal education was to be had at Billy Mitchell. Down the street was the Governor's Mansion. Garrison Keillor lived around the corner and it was a hop, skip, and a jump to the downtown.

Pulling up to the curb, Jack checked the street number and confirmed that he had the right place. A set of stone steps lead to an enclosed porch that fronted the large brick home. The ancient doorbell brought a tall thin woman to the door. Identifying herself as Adde, she invited him into the large foyer, which was crowned by an enormous open staircase. Jack followed her into the foyer.

According to Adde, her grandmother rarely ventured past the upstairs anymore. Age limited her mobility, but her mind was "still sharp." She received visitors in her upstairs sitting room. "Follow me please," Adde instructed. They ascended the wide staircase to the mid-level landing. Jack stopped and stared at the black and white photo that hung on the wall.

"She's beautiful," he said to no one in particular.

"Why thank you," a voice came from the top of the stairs. Adde and Jack both turned and looked up to find Tippy Gamble peering down at them from the banister.

"I've been expecting you Mr. Delaney. Please. Come up," Tippy turned away from the railing.

She was seated in a chair by a tall open window. Age and arthritis had done its work, but her eyes were the same bewitching ones in the picture. He noticed that her hair was dyed and her nails were done. Dressed in satin, her makeup was done up, and the sweet smell of "White Shoulders" perfume reminded him of the widow.

"I understand that the purpose of your visit is to bring me something from Rebecca's estate. I simply cannot imagine what it might be. You know, Rebecca and I had not spoken in eons."

"Yes Ma'am. It's a picture of Mr. Fitzgerald." Jack retrieved the framed photo from his worn briefcase and handed it to her. Silence followed a sigh as Tippy took it gently from his hand and placed it in her lap.

"I want to thank you young man. Mr. Fitzgerald and I were very dear friends. I knew him since we were children." She sat the picture on the table next to her alongside a small crystal vase filled with fresh pansies. Within her reach was an ancient fan and a hand mirror with an ivory handle. Tippy invited Jack to sit down.

"Your name is familiar to me Mr. Delaney. I understand that you have something to do with the police business and that you were Rebecca's caretaker."

"Yes Ma'am. For the better part of twenty five years I took care of the place and helped out Mrs. Fitzgerald. I'm a retired cop," he confirmed.

"You know that we were not close," she said. "At least not in our later years. I'm sure you understand. It is one of those unfortunate misunderstandings that come between people." This explained why Jack had never heard about Tippy Gamble.

"She treated me very well," he said. "I miss her."

Mrs. Gamble asked Adde to get something cool for them to drink. After delivering two tall glasses of iced lemonade Adde excused herself and closed the door leaving the two of them alone.

"My husband, John Gamble, was a very successful businessman. He left me comfortable in my old age and he provided wonderfully for me when he was still alive," she said with authority. She was accustomed to giving direction and was comfortable as the absolute center of attention.

"Rebecca married a man who was a failure. While I loved Thomas with all my heart, I knew from childhood that he probably would not amount to much. He was just too wooly headed to ever accomplish anything of importance. His head was always in the clouds," she said, pausing to sip of her lemonade.

"He was born with a wonderfully large silver spoon in his mouth, but could never parlay that into a successful life. I see that you are a bit surprised Mr. Delaney. I suppose my cousin bored you about the ultimate greatness of her husband. She was a fool. A silly fool. The difference in our husbands' stations in life was a constant source of irritation and jealousy on Rebecca's part. I suppose that I didn't help matters. But I refuse to apologize for my good fortune and I was not about to hide it. Believe you me, if the shoe had been on the other foot she would have held it over me." She paused again for a long sip this time and then lit a cigarette before continuing. "Rumor had it that Thomas was really not a very good lawyer. I know that he had an eye for the ladies which was always a distraction. When he was not engaged in that game, he could be found reading poetry instead of his law books. His name carried him as far as he went," she concluded. Tippy revealed that she had begun her close friendship with Thomas at an early age. As they matured into adulthood, Tippy became his lifelong confidant.

"Our mothers were sisters. We lived in St. Paul and Rebecca lived in Brunswick. We visited often and I became good friends with Thomas and Mattie Beret. Thomas was resigned that he would end up like his father in law and politics. While he knew it was the path chosen for him, the thought repulsed him. He felt trapped and knew that his love for poetry and the arts would be his avocation, but not his vocation," Tippy took a couple of deep drags and blew the smoke out the side of her mouth away from him.

"I suppose you are wondering why I tell you all of this. Especially since we are perfect strangers," taking another drag on the cigarette, adding "I want you to understand the significance of the picture you brought me. There is a story behind it that has been waiting to be told for a long time. Would you like to hear it," she asked. Continuing she said, "I feel its time to unburden myself with this story. Fortunately or not for you, you are the one who is going to hear it." A breeze blew into the open window. Its coolness cut through the room the same way truth slices through a lie.

# CHAPTER THIRTY FIVE

Tippy began her story with her favorite subject, herself. Winifred had been named for her maternal grandmother. Because of little Winifred's propensity for knocking everything under the sun over, her father began to call her Tippy. The name stuck and no one ever called her Winifred again.

She was well acquainted with Brunswick from her frequent visits with Rebecca's family. Even though Rebecca seemed old-fashioned and prudish, she was Tippy's favorite cousin. They had wonderful times and it was always a let down when she had to return to St. Paul. She attended parties given by her aunt, learned how to shoot pool on the billiard table in the large third floor game room, and became friends with Rebecca's friends. If the truth were known, she lost her virginity along the banks of Dismal Creek to a boy bearing a striking resemblance to Thomas Fitzgerald.

On most visits, Tippy gathered with Rebecca, Mattie Beret, and Thomas Fitzgerald who all lived in the prestigious Third Ward of the city. Lumber barons had originally built the huge mansions along the banks of the river and the neighborhood reeked of privilege and wealth.

Mattie Beret set her sights on Thomas Fitzgerald at an early age. So it came as a surprise to Tippy when Mattie began to speak about an older country boy who delivered wood to the Beret household. "I simply could not understand why Mattie would be interested in an errand boy," Tippy said. "It still perplexes me."

This errand boy was so far below them in class as to be invisible, especially considering the station of the Beret family. Judge Henry Beret was the most well respected man in the city. A man of impeccable rectitude and propriety, he was president of every board he ever sat on and he chaired every committee to which he was ever assigned. People who mattered, like city fathers, financiers, and businessmen, literally hung on every word spoken by the judge. Handsome, brilliant, and well spoken, Judge Henry Beret was quite a man.

Befitting such a man, he married money which bought a life of financial ease and social responsibility. Wealth bought the stately mansion located at the corner of State Street and Summit Avenue in the heart of the Third Ward. The Beret house was special even by the lofty standards of the privileged few who lived in that area. Wealth provided entrée into the circles of power and gave the judge access to the city's innermost circle.

Tippy dismissed Mattie's romantic musings as an adolescent lark. No one entertained serious thought that this would develop into anything beyond a mere fantasy.

One Christmas vacation brought a thick blanket of heavy snow and an extended visit to Rebecca's. Every day, the gang, as they called themselves, went skiing on Bob's Knob. It was actually known as Robert's Hill, but no one called it that unless they were from out of town.

For Christmas the gang had all received skiing equipment, the latest stuff ordered from New York. Skiing was the rage of the rich.

They took full advantage of the snow and of the skiing lessons of-fered at The Knob and were soon scooting down the hill at break neck speed.

On one particular morning, with skis over their shoulders, they trooped out of Mattie's driveway on their way to The Knob. Reed thin and tall for his age, Thomas towered above the girls. Witty and charming, he impressed the girls with his patter and his panache. Walt Whitman was his favorite poet and he loved to recite the lines from "O Captain! My Captain!" and "When Lilacs Last in the Dooryard Bloom'd," both poems about the death of Lincoln. Thomas loved the melancholy figure of Abraham Lincoln and was fascinated by the relationship be-tween Lincoln and Whitman. The poet and politician, crossing paths in Civil War Washington D.C.

Civil War Washington was a sweltering fetid disease ridden swamp. Lincoln, to avoid the heat and to get away from the war, stayed at the Soldier's Home. It was located on high, cool, breezy ground. During the day he toiled in the executive mansion. At night, he would ride his horse out to the old Soldier's Home. His route often took him near the little cottage that Walt Whitman called home. The two men would tip their hats and bow their heads to each other as Lincoln passed by. When the great man fell, Whitman wept, letting his tears flow through poetic words.

Thomas developed a deep love for the two men and their con-nection to history. Impressing the girls once again with his rendi-tion of "O Captain! My Captain!" they marched arm in arm and ski to shoulder down the Beret driveway. Up the Beret driveway came the errand boy. Tippy had never seen a team of horses that big up that close. They pulled an enormous sled loaded with blocks of split wood. Driving the team with the confidence of a man was a broad shouldered, serious looking boy. The errand boy's clothing said all that was needed about the gulf in their respective social places. He wore drab, worn woolens with his hat tipped slightly to one side the way a person would raise an eyebrow in a moment of attitude. The reigns were held by a pair of large gloved hands. His voice was firm and the horses responded accordingly.

"Hayseed," Thomas said as Will Graves passed them with the team. Mattie admonished them and refused to join in the insults.

"After we skied for an hour or so all was forgotten. Then Will Graves pulled up with his team. He strapped on his skis and made us all look like beginners. He didn't speak to us or even look our way. His point made."

Tippy and Jack took a break from the story as Adde replenished their drinks. Clearly Tippy was performing for Jack. As she told the story, Tippy would occasionally look at herself in her handheld mirror. When she was not sipping her lemonade or smoking a cigarette she would run a brush through her hair. With the break over, Tippy once again warmed to her subject.

"Mattie always stood up for the underdog. She had little patience for rudeness towards the poor. She treated everyone the same. I suppose it was that attitude that helped her see past the worn clothes and into the heart of Will Graves."

It was at the Masonic charity dance in the spring of 1943 that Tippy next saw Will Graves. They'd all been having a grand time before he showed up at the dance. All of them had a buzz on due to Thomas's unfailing ability to provide spirited drinks for every occasion. They drank hard liquor from a flask kept in the car and sipped on cream sodas at the dance. Whenever Mattie got wound up she loved to talk politics. "Father says he won't run for a fourth term."

"I wouldn't be so damn sure about that. FDR is power hungry. He'll never let go," Fitz disagreed.

"I didn't say I agreed with father. I said that he doesn't believe Franklin will run for another term," Mattie said.

"I think he's wonderful. I just love all that "you have nothing to fear but fear itself" language that he uses," Mattie added. Mattie liked to use FDR's first name as though they were intimates, Tippy said to Jack.

"I told them that I could care less if Roosevelt or Bing Crosby is president. Who cares? I just wanted to dance. Parties and not politics were my concern," she said. "Rebecca didn't understand any of it. Most of our conversations went over her head."

All of their parents were card carrying Republicans. Pro-Roosevelt talk was discouraged in their homes. "Mattie declared herself a Democrat, which of course drove her father crazy. She had a way of needling him." World affairs, politics, and business were discussed at the Beret dinner table. It was also an unfortunate fact in the Beret household that Mrs. Beret's opinion did not matter. Henry ran their lives.

Before the Masonic dance, Thomas told Tippy that he was going to propose marriage to Mattie at his next opportunity. Although he was nervous like all young men about to propose marriage, he was not doubtful about the outcome.

"We danced to Glen Miller's 'In the Mood', my favorite song." Tippy said with a smile as she remembered the moment. "I love the part where music dies down and goes soft for a number of beats before exploding."

That evening's dance belonged to Thomas Fitzgerald and Mattie Beret. Both were particularly good dancers and they captivated the attention of all present as they cut loose. For the span of a dance they were united as a couple and totally merged in a way they would never be again. Mattie and Fitz were lost in each other as they whirled and swirled and dipped and dived. Hand in hand they made their way back to the table at the close of the dance. Then their lives changed forever.

"Excuse me, I think I see an old friend," and with that, Mattie Beret walked out of Thomas Fitzgerald's life and into Will Graves'. Leaning against the wall was a sailor with his hat tipped in attitude.

"Horrified. That's what everyone felt. We all felt horrified. Mattie married the errand boy. Thomas was crushed. He never recovered. From then until his death his heart was broken. Mattie was disowned by her father."

Tippy's glass was empty. Adde was summoned by the ringing of a small bell.

"I hope I am not boring you Mr. Delaney," Tippy said mock serious.

"Not at all ma'am," he replied. "It's fascinating. I had no idea."

"Maybe we should call it a day," Adde suggested. She had returned to check on Tippy. With some gentle persuasion Adde convinced her grandmother to resume the next day. Jack rose and shook hands with Tippy who remained seated. He had to lean forward in order to take her hand and as he did so he caught a whiff of alcohol.

On the way out, Jack once again paused on the stairs to admire Tippy's beauty inside the picture frame.

# CHAPTER THIRTY SIX

Anna sat reading in the alcove. According to her grandmother's journals, she never got over the estrangement with her father. Anna read that her great grandmother had initially disagreed with Mattie's decision to marry Will Graves. She relented when it became clear that Mattie would marry him with or without her blessing. However, Mattie would have to persuade her formidable father. Mattie had challenged her father on a few occasions without much success. But there had never been a confrontation over a subject so substantial. Henry Beret was not a man to be trifled with under any circumstances. He was used to getting his way.

Judge Beret showed his strength in different ways. Once a hobo had attempted to assault Mattie as she walked home from a Job's Daughters meeting. At the time, Henry Beret served as Brunswick County District Attorney. Henry saw to it that the perpetrator went to prison for a long time. On another occasion, he saved a drowning woman from the icy river. He was in his early 60s at the time.

Her biggest challenge to him thus far was when she signed up for her Army physical. Mattie presented it as a "fait accompli," but her father's influence cut the matter short. A precise contemporary journal entry gave Anna a flavor of what had occurred.

"Father, what have you done," Mattie had demanded when she learned of her father's denial of her enlistment. He sat reading and smoking in his chair.

"If you're referring to this Army business, I looked out for your best interest. You are apparently incapable of doing so," he explained.

"I am perfectly capable of watching out for myself. Father, you had no right..." Henry interrupted her at this point.

"I have every right. You are my daughter," he said in a lawyerly tone.

"I want to serve. It is my duty," Mattie said with more than a trace of heat.

"Do not raise your voice to me young lady. If you cannot discuss this matter like an adult, we will not discuss it at all. Go to your room," he commanded.

"Father..." Mattie protested.

"That's enough. Case closed." That ended the argument and dashed all of Mattie's hopes to join the Army. But the subject of marriage dwarfed the Army.

"Father I have something to tell you," Mattie said through his newspaper as he sat in his chair reading. He put down his newspaper and looked at her over the top of his reading glasses.

"What is it Mattie," he asked. Mattie at first hemmed and hawed and then spit and sputtered. But she braced herself against his firm resolve and regained her composure.

"Will Graves and I are to be married."

"Is this some kind of a joke?"

"No father. I am dead serious. I am going to marry Will Graves before he ships out." At the close of her sentence she straightened up to stand a little taller.

"Someone told me you had been talking to him," Judge Beret said.

"Well father, do I have your blessing?"

"You most certainly do not," he said. "What about Thomas." By now the paper had been tossed on the floor and Judge Beret stood facing his daughter. His question knifed through her. It touched the raw chord of guilt she felt about abandoning Thomas. When she thought of it she could no longer hold her father's gaze and she looked at the floor.

"I didn't think you were serious," her father said. Mattie looked back into his eyes.

"You're wrong father. I'm 21 years old. I'm sorry about Thomas, but I love Will Graves. I think I loved him a little even when he delivered wood to us."

"Nonsense. He was a delivery boy. What kind of life would you have with this man? Who knows if he'll even survive the war? Then what? You want to be a farmer's wife?"

"No matter what you think father I am a grown woman. I have come to ask for your blessing. Not your permission."

"Well, you have neither," with that Henry Beret walked out of the room.

At first Henry went to see Owen Graves to demand that he reason with his son. Owen was respectful and certainly empathetic to another father's plight, but he stood firm by his son. Next, Henry confronted Will Graves face to face. Owen had told Judge Beret that he could find Will out behind the barn tinkering with an old piece of machinery. Will was just as respectful as Owen, but his resolve was sound.

Henry did not take losing with grace. Mattie was informed by letter that upon her marriage to Will Graves she was to remove herself from his house and his life, forever. Her inheritance would be severed and they would never speak again. If it was a bluff, it was a big one. As a gamble it did not pay off. More than likely he meant every single word of it. Mattie packed and left.

In the years that followed, Mattie made reference to the pain she felt over the loss. The tenor of her words were angry at first, then they evolved into longing and finally into a wistful sadness. Mattie's mother continued to have a relationship with her throughout her life. She described her husband as an "old fool." Towards the end of his life, her mother described him as a bitter, lonely, decrepit old man who had brought it all upon himself by severing ties with his only child. In the process losing the respect and love of his wife.

As Mattie aged, she grew more empathetic and forgiving of her father. Her own son John had become a thin presence in her life. Putting herself in her father's shoes she wrote a poem about the loneliness and hopelessness of old age. Anna read it with a lump in her throat. She titled the poem "January Rain".

It became clear that Mattie had a confidant for a period of years during the late 40s and early 50s. Anna was convinced that this ghostly presence in her grandmother's journal was her biological grandfather. Anna was touched by the tenderness in the passages throughout the journals. Although at this point, Anna thought that learning the identity of her real grandfather was beside the point. Will Graves would always be her "Gramps." She knew that he had as much influence over her as any one except her grandmother. She was nonetheless intrigued with this unknown man who had touched her grandmother's heart. It was at this point in her reading that her water broke.

Anna drove to the hospital alone after dropping Harry off at the kennel. As usual, Jack's cell phone was off or was in his glove compartment. She couldn't leave a message anyway because Jack still didn't use his voice mail. The man is a bit of a Neanderthal, she thought. He had called from the hotel the previous evening to say that there would be a delay of one day. When she called the hotel after her water broke, they informed her that Jack had already checked out. Since there was no way to contact him, Anna left a note and set forth.

She had determined that there would be no epidural. Wanting to experience the natural birth of her child, she refused any drugs that would mar the experience. The pain of labor only intensified her resolve. Once she was settled in between labor pains, she occupied herself with her grandmother's journal which had been prepacked. Anna thought it appropriate that Mattie should be present at the birth of her great grandchild.

Anna settled in and resumed her reading. One of Mattie's pleasures had been her yard where she had spent hours. It was her space to wander and wonder and wish. Especially fond of the lilacs that adorned her yard, Mattie never failed to record a spring bloom in her journal. The barn may have been Will's safe harbor, but the yard and the lilacs belonged to Mattie. She planted them when she first came to the farm. Her mother-in-law encouraged her to "brighten up" the place.

"You know, you don't have to be hero." A middle aged nurse with a lot of babies under her belt interrupted her and advised as she checked the monitor. "Just breathe. Are you sure that you don't want that epidural," she asked once again.

"No. I am just fine thank you," Anna gritted out between clenched teeth. Mattie Anne was definitely on her way into this world. Anna couldn't wait to see her face, although she already had a good idea what she would look like. When the pain subsided, Anna returned to the journal.

# CHAPTER THIRTY SEVEN

Upon return to the house the next day, Adde motioned for Jack to follow her to Tippy's room. Adde plied them with strong coffee and left them alone. Sipping his coffee, Jack relaxed into the chair as Tippy resumed her story.

According to Tippy, Fitz's reluctance to join the military had a profound impact on Mattie's view of him as a man. While he did everything he could to avoid the prospect of service, Mattie worked at joining. Tippy concluded that "Fitz was a coward." With his father's help, Fitz worked the levers of power until he got an appointment to a civilian position with the defense department. The thing that infuriated Mattie the most was his lack of shame.

The argument caused Fitz to retreat to St. Paul. Whenever Fitz had to lick a wound, he always found solace in Tippy's presence and had related the blowup to her. She recounted the gist of the argument.

"It is our duty to serve not shirk," Mattie argued.

"Mattie, listen to me, there is more than one way to contribute. Not everyone must live in a foxhole," he countered. Adding, "I'll be better used in my position at the defense department."

His attempt to persuade her on the merits failed. Mattie ended the argument by telling him she would never forgive him for his cowardliness. It was the one area of contention that was never reconciled between them. Tippy believed that it was this incident that sealed his fate with Mattie. The contrast between Fitz and Will could not have been clearer.

"I suppose I can be forgiven for my selfishness. I never thought ill of Fitz for his yellow streak. If he had gone off to war and gotten killed, I would have lost my playmate. There was simply no one else with his conversational flare. We connected intellectually and socially," Tippy said.

"It's a shame about Mr. Fitzgerald's accident," Jack mentioned as Adde swapped full cups for empty ones and left them alone again. Picking up the brush again, Tippy stroked her hair in her absentminded way. After looking at herself in the ancient mirror she fixed her gaze upon Jack.

"Accident? Mr. Delaney, Fitz's death was no accident. He killed himself." Letting Jack recover from the shock for a few beats, Tippy resumed. "Have you heard of the poem called "Richard Cory" by Edwin Arlington Robinson?"

Jack had no idea what some poem had to do with Thomas Fitzgerald's death, but he went along anyway.

"Richard Cory was a dandy. An aristocrat. He lived in a big house in what appeared to be a perfect world. All who looked upon him were jealous of his wealth and status. And then, Mr. Delaney, as the poem says, 'he went home and put a bullet through his head.' Yes, my detective friend, Thomas committed suicide."

"This arrived after his death," she handed Jack a book of poems. "It was mailed the day he died." It was a book of Robinson poetry with "Richard Cory" marked with a folded piece of paper. Jack opened up the paper and read "Sorry. Fitz."

"Well I'll be damned. He killed himself. No one ever knew that. No one suspected suicide. The widow...sorry, Mrs. Fitzgerald, never ever said anything about a suicide. Did she know," Jack asked.

Tippy smiled at Jack's characterization of her cousin as "The Widow." She could certainly see why someone would end up calling her that, considering she wore it as a mantel.

"Of course she knew, Mr. Delaney. She covered it up. In fact, Rebecca blamed me for his death. My cousin was not a smart woman, but even she could sense that her husband was cheating on her. She thought it was me that had broken his heart and he had killed himself as a result."

"What made her think you were the one," Jack asked.

"I suppose our closeness had something to do with it. Thomas and I spent oodles of time together over the years. Like I say she was not the smartest person in the world. It was the easiest conclusion for her to draw. It was not Rebecca's habit to look deeply into things," she explained. "She requested that I not attend his funeral. I honored her request. Although I made my own pilgrimage there when the time was right," she added.

"Did you have any idea that Mr. Fitzgerald was in this state of mind and would possibly take his life?"

"Why of course I did. Whenever Thomas was blue about love, he played with death. After Mattie married another man his broken heart never healed. She was the direct cause of his suffering. No, I would say I wasn't surprised. Sad, but not surprised at all," she said.

"Mrs. Fitzgerald made him out to be some kind of a god. She was convinced he would have made a fine governor or something like that. Why would she do that?"

"My, my, Mr. Delaney, you really have no idea about my cousin, do you?"

According to Tippy, Rebecca Moore had seen herself as the first lady of the land from the time she was a little girl. Smitten by Fitz's ebullience and literary flare, Rebecca just knew he would make a fine president of the United States. And everyone, including Fitz, knew that he was slated for the family business of law and politics. But anyone with a lick of sense could see that the boy's natural disposition was elsewhere.

"I could always find him out at Dismal Creek writing poetry or daydreaming. He was way too soft to be successful in politics. Rebecca simply could not see reality through the fog of her own pipe dream."

So when Mattie married Will Graves, Rebecca made herself available. Bleeding from his heart, Fitz fell into the first set of arms that were open. Those arms happened to belong to Rebecca Moore. With almost no effort on her part, Rebecca had her dream and her man, Tippy explained.

"Hollow was her victory, Mr. Delaney, misery became her life. There was no keeping Thomas Fitzgerald home. Fitz attracted women like a magnet. In public, Thomas treated Rebecca with respect. At home he ignored her. Rebecca spent their early years trying to get pregnant. But after a series of miscarriages and false starts, she finally gave up amidst Thomas's indifference. When it became apparent that she was unable to conceive, she turned to Thomas's political career. Playing host at numerous dinner parties kept Rebecca busy for several years. Fitz was an affable, if unenthusiastic accomplice in the effort."

Tippy confided that while everyone liked Thomas and most were charmed by him, it was obvious to the old hands that Thomas was not much of a politician. There was no fire in the belly. He managed to get elected to the state senate. But after two terms, Thomas and the voters mutually agreed to go their separate ways.

Fitz had concluded that since he could not have Mattie, and he did not want Rebecca, he would have to have his needs met in other ways. A succession of casual affairs ruled his love life. Doing little except sleeping in his own home, the sharing of the marital bed became nonexistent. Still, Rebecca clung to her delusions. Because appearances had to be maintained at all costs, Rebecca covered up the fact that Thomas had killed himself.

Tippy told Jack that the only ray of sunshine in Thomas Fitzgerald's life was Mattie Beret Graves. It was only on those rare occasions when he was included in her life, that he seemed truly happy. During those brief intervals over the years when they would see each other, Fitz would refrain from all other casual relationships. Their rare and sporadic rendezvous were sprinkled over a period of years. And when they finally stopped altogether, Fitz gave up on life.

"Are you alright, Mr. Delaney," Tippy leaned forward putting her hand on his arm. "You look pale. I suppose you were shocked to learn that Mattie and Fitz were lovers."

"Yes Ma'am. I guess you could say I'm at a loss for words. It's just...that...."

"Well, Mattie was quite a spectacular woman. I'll give you that. She was the only woman that I ever felt threatened by. She was the only woman that could ever hold her own with me." Tippy thought for a moment and then added "strictly on the beauty side, I think I had her beat. Mattie's beauty was elegant and classic. I had a little more spice." Jack found it hard to disagree on that point.

"Mr. Delaney you should be mature enough to realize that all of us carry around a little baggage. Even Mattie, as perfect as she was, could not escape the vagaries of life. Life's bumpy. Wouldn't you agree?"

"I suppose so Ma'am. Still, it's quite a shocker." Jack was not shocked that Mattie had an affair, but he was stunned that it was with Thomas Fitzgerald.

"Let's break for lunch Mr. Delaney. After which I will fill you in on the details."

# CHAPTER THIRTY EIGHT

After the last wave of pain subsided, Anna again tried Jack's cell phone. Failing to reach him she turned once again to the journals. Teaching was the central aspect of Mattie Beret's life, and her love for it shown like a beacon. Anna loved that aspect of her grandmother. It was clear that Mattie was most proud of her teaching ability over anything else she had ever done.

As the journal revealed, life as she knew it changed dramatically following her marriage to Will Graves. They barely had time to consummate the union before Will shipped out to the Pacific, leaving her in unfamiliar territory. She lived in a strange house with strangers and had entered a strange life. Her only anchor in a drifting sea was her connection to teaching.

Her love of school, books, learning, and teaching was cemented on her first day in school when she was six years old. Her mother walked her to the school which was only a few blocks from their home. Mattie's initial excitement was interpreted as nervousness and her mother asked her if she was scared. Mattie replied that she was not, asking if her mother thought she was a little kid.

Mattie's intelligence and aptitude was immediately apparent. This translated into her ability to skip a grade. One of her teachers even had her write out spelling tests because she always got 100%. School and teaching became her life, then and there.

It wasn't long after settling on the farm that she filled an opening at Maple Drive School. It was the same one room schoolhouse that her husband had attended. All eight elementary grades were taught in that one room. When it came time for a lesson, that particular class would assemble in a half-circle of chairs at the front of the room. Mattie would teach the lesson and then the next group would come up for their turn. In the meantime, the remaining students would stay in their seats and study.

Mattie taught all of the local kids including Jack Delaney, Doyle Howland, and Cindy Robertson. Anna had been pleasantly surprised to find a reference to Jack in Mattie's papers. She described him as pleasant, somewhat aloof, and serious. Her journals were sprinkled with comments about her students, good and bad.

Although Mattie loved teaching, she hated tending the wood stove and hauling water from the outdoor pump. She was elated when offered the high school English teaching position. In her new role, she could indulge her love of poetry. She liked to paraphrase Robert Frost that life should be a melding of one's passion and profession. For Mattie, teaching fulfilled that role.

She had numerous letters and cards from former students thanking her for the difference that she had made in their lives. She strove to make literature relevant. In-class discussions of poetry and prose were filled with references to real life. She wove images and themes about love, honor, courage, duty, and the sweet pain of life into her lessons. Mattie found the poetry of Robert Frost to be particularly suited to her teaching philosophy. She loved his observational astuteness about seemingly small matters. He was at once serious and playful as he turned the mundane into the philosophical.

Her favorite example was illustrated in the poem "Nothing Gold Can Stay." She used that poem to illustrate that life moves fast and that opportunities all slip away eventually. Her goal was to awaken a sense of urgency in the young lives who passed through her classroom. "How can there be an appreciation of life, if one is unaware of its impermanence," she would rhetorically ask.

While Mattie loved teaching and would not have done anything else, it was by no means an easy job. There were numerous references in her journals to long days and the frustrations of not getting through to her students. On these occasions, Mattie would relax in a hot bath after a long day at school. She would luxuriate in steaming perfumed water as she listened to Billie Holiday. She referred to the episodes as her "pleasure" baths, wistfully recording her longing to have someone read love poetry to her as she soaked and relaxed. She made passing reference to Whitman's poetic eroticism as the type she wanted to hear.

# CHAPTER THIRTY NINE

After lunch Tippy and Jack remained on the porch as Adde cleared the table and plied them with strong coffee. It was a welcome change from the champagne which had left him dizzy. Tippy did not appear affected in the least. The woman could hold her booze and without missing a beat, she resumed her tale.

In yet another attempt to further her husband's political career, Rebecca planned yet another dinner. Tippy and her husband were invited. The event coincided with the annual fair where Thomas was to introduce the governor as part of the festivities.

As long as the big shots were gathered in Brunswick, a soiree was in order. Fitz was one of many standing for office that year. While Tippy was truly apolitical, it was great theater and she loved a good show.

Most of the assembled politicians were a collective bore. The core of their conversation was about how to get elected, how to stay elected, and once elected how to use their power to repeat the process over and over again. But it was not the content of the discussions that interested Tippy.

"I found the hypocrites themselves fascinating," she said. "Men plotted against other men in the same room. At the same time they smiled and shook hands and back slapped and promised loyalty. But the wives were the worst. To be sure the men were two-faced. That was just politics. But the wives were believers. Rebecca among them. Because the dinner followed the fair, everyone first gathered at the fairgrounds in the early afternoon to hear the speeches," she explained.

A hot, humid July day greeted the fair goers. With the war over people had returned to their lives with great intensity. A day at the fair was one of those "pursuit of happiness" things they had fought a war to preserve. Music, food, rides, exhibits, and speakers lent a carefree festive air to the gathering.

Tippy and her husband wandered through prize winning baking and sewing exhibits. John Gamble won his wife a prize in the arcade and took her on the Ferris wheel. They ate cotton candy and visited the barns to admire the horses. Before they gathered with the rest of the group they licked homemade ice cream cones under the shade of an oak tree. Then it was time for the speeches.

All of the speakers said nothing in their own mediocre way. Tippy was never less inspired by so many words in her life. My God, Tippy told Jack, if the people did not demand more than what this bunch offered, they deserved what they got. Fitz was at least funny.

With the speeches over, they rose to go. Rebecca had earlier been escorted home by Tippy's husband right after Fitz's introduction of the governor. She needed to attend to last minute details and wanted to be there to greet the guests as they arrived. As Tippy walked with Fitz to the car, they ran into Mattie Graves. Mattie had been in the grandstands listening to the speeches and was making her way through the crowd when she bumped into Tippy.

"Oh, excuse me," Mattie said when she collided with Tippy. Then recognition and surprise registered at once. "Tippy! Oh my

God, how are you?" The women embraced and then the three of them got out of the way of the jostling crowd.

"Mattie, how nice to see you," Tippy replied, then looked at Thomas. He looked as though he had seen a ghost. Enduring an awkward moment, Thomas stretched out his hand to shake Mattie's, who returned the gesture. She also gave him a quick hug and then praised his speech.

"Did you really like it?"

"Of course. It was wonderful. How's your campaign going? I see your signs everywhere."

Mattie had had no contact with Fitz since the night of the Masonic dance, but she was aware of Fitz's life through Rebecca, staying friends and in close contact with her. Although Mattie never went to her house, Rebecca often visited the farm.

Tippy could see the pain of this moment in Fitz's eyes and in his uneasy manner. Normally Fitz was fluid in his movements, but at the moment seemed unable to find a place for his hands. His easy charm had been transformed into tongue tied awkwardness. Letting Fitz off the hook, the two women chatted. They caught up on gossip and all had a soda at the nearby concession stand.

According to Tippy, Mattie looked beautiful in her flowered yellow sun dress and hat. She was tan from tending her garden and her young body was in full bloom. Fitz did not look so bad himself in his dark blue double breasted suit. His tall frame had filled out some and he looked every inch a professional man. Men and women glanced at them as they walked by. Two beautiful women escorted by a tall handsome well dressed man was bound to cause a little commotion at a county fair. Tippy loved the attention and would often return the men's glances causing them embarrassment. She was married, not dead, she explained to Jack. Besides she added, her husband saw it as a source of power and pride to have a trophy wife like Tippy.

On the drive from the fairgrounds, Fitz made a short detour to a secluded spot along Dismal Creek where a grassy peninsula was surrounded by tall white pines. Fitz fell sobbing into Tippy's arms and she held him until the sobs subsided. When he regained his composure, Fitz and Tippy continued to his home in silence.

For the rest of the evening Fitz wandered among the guests in a daze. Tippy stayed close and acted as proxy when Fitz drifted off to the quiet corners of the garden or wandered into his private library. She would gently persuade him to return to his guests even when he would say "To hell with them." As usual, Rebecca was oblivious to anything but the pursuit of her own pipe dream.

Not long after that day at the fair, Fitz came to St. Paul to once again lick his wounds. Fitz moved into the guest bedroom and spent his days on the upstairs porch staring into space. Whenever he pulled himself up far enough to see beyond his despair, he would let alcohol wash him back into a black hole. According to Tippy, Fitz eventually crawled back to reality. At the end of his stay, Fitz wrote the first of his letters to Mattie asking her to meet him.

"I can't stand it anymore. If she won't see me then...well...there's not much use to being around," Fitz explained his reason for the letter. It was not the first time he had suggested suicide as a way out.

"If Mattie would have you, would you divorce Rebecca," Tippy had asked at the time.

"I'd give up everything, and I mean everything, if she would come back to me. My career, my marriage, my self-respect—everything. But, there's no chance of that. So I'd settle for just seeing her once in a while." When he left St. Paul he was determined to send the letter no matter the consequence. Tippy did not hear from him for a while, but then he called, jubilant.

"She's going to meet me. Can you believe it," Fitz said over the phone. Promising to keep her updated, Fitz went to his destiny.

Within days Fitz was back in St. Paul. This time he was on top of the world.

Mattie had met him at Dismal Creek. Mattie was very reserved, but she promised to think about another meeting. Tippy and Fitz hit the bottle in celebration.

It was not long before Fitz and Mattie advanced from talk to intimacy. For about a year their affair consumed them both, then stopped cold. Mattie insisted that they end the affair immediately. Her conscience had gotten the better of her.

Once again, a drunken, tortured Fitz produced another letter while at Tippy's. She remembered that Fitz pleaded for Mattie to reconsider. He then surprised Mattie at a Robert Frost Society meeting in Madison. When she returned to her room at the Concourse Hotel, a message was waiting. If she so desired, Fitz could be found in the hotel bar. This time Mattie relented and agreed to go with him to the room he kept while the Legislature was in session.

Fitz confided to Tippy that while Mattie soaked in his big claw foot bathtub, he played Billie Holiday records and read Walt Whitman to her. Besides poems on the death of President Lincoln, Whitman penned serious erotic rhyme, Tippy explained to Jack, repeating what Fitz had told her about it.

It was an enchanting night for them both. Fitz reminisced often over the years about that evening's magic. Generally, Fitz was very discreet about details of his affairs including the one with Mattie. However, this evening was special and he did describe some of it to Tippy.

"God help me for telling you this. But it's a night I'll never forget," Fitz had said. "I fell asleep. When I woke up it was dark. Mattie sat in the chair smoking as she looked out at the Capitol. Its reflected light was her only cover. I swear to God I've never seen a more beautiful sight in my life," he added.

The next time Fitz called Tippy it was to inform her that he was going to be a father. Flights of fancy overtook him. He was sure that Mattie would leave Will Graves and they could be together with their child. For months it was all he could talk about. He even went so far as to retain a Madison divorce attorney in anticipation of dumping Rebecca. Jack Delaney interrupted Tippy at this point.

"How was he so sure that he was the father?"

Tippy paused and smiled at Jack. "My dear Mr. Delaney, a woman knows these things. Mattie would not have said so if it had not been true," she said. Then she picked up Fitz's picture and handed it to Jack.

"You must see the similarity between Fitz and John Graves in this picture." As Jack looked over the picture he had to admit that they looked an awful lot alike. In truth, he had never seen the resemblance before. But upon further reflection, he realized John Graves looked nothing like Will and a whole bunch like Thomas Fitzgerald. After studying the photo for a while longer he placed it back on the table next to Tippy.

"Well, I'll be. Mr. Fitzgerald was John Graves' father and Anna's grandfather. Anna will be fascinated with this. What happened next," Jack asked.

"Well, of course Mattie was not about to leave Will Graves. So once again Fitz was disappointed and forlorn. He absolutely longed to be that baby's father in every single way. Mattie refused all offers for help. Her only concession was to let Fitz see the boy a few times when he was very young," Tippy explained. "Other than that, Fitz watched his son grow up from a distance. And Mattie made him promise on his life that he would not contact John and reveal this information in any way. He was to keep this information to himself or she would never forgive him. With great effort, he kept his promise."

"What about Will Graves? Did he ever find out," Jack asked.

"Not directly. I mean that no one actually told him. However, there was one curious incident."

Once again Tippy lit a cigarette and took a deep drag. Before continuing she looked admiringly at herself in the mirror turning her face first to the left and then to the right while maintaining eye contact with herself in her reflection. She continued the story without looking away.

"One day as Fitz was reading poetry out at Dismal Creek, I believe it was something dark and foreboding by Poe, Will Graves showed up. Apparently, Fitz had been so preoccupied that he had not heard Will Graves approach. Startled, he looked up from his book to see the big man standing about 10 feet away from him. Will stared at Fitz deliberately for a few moments, an eternity to Fitz, then Will turned and walked away down the bank of the creek with his fishing pole in hand," finally she turned to Jack. "It scared Fitz half to death."

Tippy went on to explain that Fitz always carried his revolver when he went to the creek or other remote parts of the county or when traveling. She was sure that Fitz would have used it to protect himself against Will Graves if it had become necessary. "It was that yellow streak, you know. Fitz swore that the look given to him by Will Graves was filled with knowledge and hatred. However, other than this one time there were no other indications that he knew," she said.

Jack could take it no longer. He had to ask about the murder. It was the elephant in the room and if this woman had any knowledge about it, now was the time for it to be revealed. His sixth sense was working overtime and he believed that he was closer to solving the murder of Sonny Howland than at any time in his life.

"Does any of this have anything to do with the murder of Sonny Howland?"

Tippy took another drink of lemonade, once again passed the brush through her hair, and then sitting back smiled at Jack Delaney. Exhaling her smoke, she said "I was wondering when you'd get around to asking that question."

# CHAPTER FORTY

After another round of pain, a doctor's exam, a nurse's reassur-
ance, and one more unanswered cell phone call to Jack, Anna
re-read the last letter from her grandmother. Much of the letter was
filled with Mattie's philosophy on life which could be distilled down to
the golden rule. She believed in tolerance toward her fellow human
beings, but possessed no utopian outlook on mankind. According to
Mattie, people had both good and bad in them.

She said, "There's not so much good in someone that you won't
find some bad and no one is so bad that you won't find a little
good." She attempted to apply this human trait to herself by revealing one of her own deficiencies.

She wrote, "I am sure you would be shocked to learn that your
grandmother smoked cigarettes most of her adult life. It has been
my practice to conceal my cigarette smoking because I like to keep
some things to myself. Even though I know I am being dishonest
about the existence of this habit." Mattie then referred Anna to
the Robert Frost poem about the secret that "sits in the middle and
knows." Anna had to agree with Mattie that Sir Robert had great
insight into the human heart.

Mattie also had a realistic view point on her marriage which she chose to share with Anna. The problem with most marriages is failed expectations, she reasoned. Tolerance and acceptance of one's spouse and their respective shortcomings produced stable marriages, she counseled Anna. "No man is perfect. Even the best like your grandfather. After all, they are just men and they will never understand the female no matter how many thousands of years we exist together. Take your grandfather for instance. He was the most wonderful man and the most wonderful husband. But he was totally unable to express his love and deepest feelings to me or to anyone. He had very little romance in his nature. Even so, I accepted him and did not try and change his behavior. I was simply tolerant of it while I wished that he could have been more open." Her grandmother had wanted Anna to understand and to have a "feel" for who her grandparents were as people, not just grandparents. Then, Mattie added a request.

"Someday you will come into possession of our farm. As you know, your father does not want any part of this place. While it pains me to accept that, I am not going to dwell on it, but rather pin my hopes on you. It is a natural wish for the old to attempt to bestow one's legacy upon the young. Both your grandfather and I would be pleased to know that you end up living here.

This much I can tell you. Living here has been a most wonderful experience. Long graceful summer days have been framed by the beauty of spring and the crispness of fall. Winter's magic has slowed time and allowed space to read and linger by a warm fire. It has been my good fortune and pleasure to have spent my life under the giant trees and among the graceful hills of this wonderful little valley. Your grandfather brought me here when I was still a very young woman. As the years passed I have watched the mirror change my face into an old woman. That change has reflected a long life lived as honestly as life can allow.

Here I have spent my life as a married woman to a truly honorable man. No one ever worked harder at doing the right thing than Will Graves. He could be a hard man when provoked, but with rare exception, his life was spent in the gentle rhythm of the land. Without exception he always lent a hand whenever and wherever it was needed. He loved this place. His great-grandfather homesteaded it in the 1860s. His father built the house in which we still live. Your grandfather watched the barn being built by his father and his grandfather when he was a young boy.

The barn he watched being built was the same one that you came to know. The same barn where you chased kittens in the hay mow and jumped off the wooden beams into the soft hay below. It is the same barn that went up in the fire.

When that happened, it broke your grandfather's heart. He talked often about watching the barn burn. He told me how the wooden beams in the barn were taken from the old St. Mary's church just down the road when the new one was built. Nothing was wasted in those days and so they re-used the beams to build the barn. Your grandfather would often joke that the holiest place on the farm was the barn because it was protected by the Virgin Mary.

As a farmer, your grandfather excelled. His fences were always perfect. The buildings shone. All the machinery ran like a top. The fields were tended and they produced wonderful crops. But he derived his greatest pleasure out of tending his cattle in that big barn. His herd was most certainly one of the best in the county. In fact, he spent more time in that barn with those cattle than with anything else, including me. All his life he studied dairy science. Whenever the university extension offered a course, he signed up. He took great pride as a farmer.

Of all the buildings on the farm, it was the barn that received the most attention. Now mind you, I did not spend much time in the barn. Although there were times when I found myself there for one reason or another, it did not happen very often. I remember that it was clean with the walkways swept and limed. The walls were whitewashed and fresh bedding was always spread out under the cows. He kept the cows clean by currying and brushing them on a daily basis. Many times over the years, your grandfather received awards from the creamery for his operation.

So here is my request of you. When the time comes for you to live here, I wish for you to have the barn rebuilt in your grandfather's memory. If it comes to pass that you are unable or unwilling to do so, I'll accept that as well. Please consider this the last wish from a foolish old woman. But it would be a wonderful tribute to your grandfather if it could happen."

It was clear to Anna that her grandmother had become very tender and caring towards her husband as he aged. His mental decline actually drew her closer to him. When he was initially diagnosed with dementia, Mattie wrote a poem in his honor.

It touched Anna that her grandmother had grown nostalgic and sentimental towards her grandfather in old age. It had been painful for Mattie to watch Will slowly lose his mind. In the last few years he had a perpetual lost look on his face. Mattie would patiently listen to him repeat himself over and over and over about the most mundane things. When it was suggested by the doctor that Will should be placed in a nursing home, Mattie refused. She was determined that she would care for him to his last breath and she kept that promise.

Putting away her grandmother's writings, Anna made herself as comfortable as possible. While she was not afraid, Anna could not help wishing that Jack was present to offer support. It was beginning to grow dark outside. Night was coming on and surely he would be arriving soon. Momentarily she felt a panic rise in her chest as she wondered if something had happened to him. Why on earth was this trip taking so long, she asked herself. He must be learning a great deal to be delayed for this length of time, she reasoned.

Her exhaustion was beginning to show and it was taking all of her energy to get through the labor. Sucking on ice chips, Anna concluded that she did indeed have a "feel" for her grandparents. The essence of her grandmother was that she had a poet's heart.

As far as her grandfather was concerned, his life had been lived with a rock solid steadiness. He had kept his disappointments to himself. His course through life had been right down the middle of the road, a man of his word in thought and deed. Theirs had been the love story of a farmer and a city girl. It had not been perfect, but it had surely been grand. She missed them both.

As Anna lay waiting for the next labor pain, she thought about her biological grandfather. She wondered if she would ever know who he was or what difference it would make in her life. Then the anticipated pain took over once again and forced her mind to the task at hand. She silently pleaded with Jack to please get here on time.

# CHAPTER FORTY ONE

E vening was upon them and Jack began to worry about his extended absence from Anna, not having contact for twenty four hours. But since he was going to stay until the end of the story no matter what, there was not much he could do about it at the moment. They relocated to Tippy's sitting room. She began the final chapter of her story with a sip of Irish coffee, a drag off a slim menthol, and one more admiring glance in the mirror.

"In some respects Mr. Delaney, I have been waiting to tell this story my entire adult life. Now it appears that...I...I have been merely waiting for the perfect audience which appears to be you." Another sip. "Where shall I begin," she asked. Then began.

During the summer of 1950 Fitz and Mattie saw each other sporadically. They met at Dismal Creek where Fitz often went to read poetry.

Throughout the summer, Mattie kept telling him that the time had come to end the affair once and for all. No good could come from the relationship, she argued. They should be satisfied with what they had been given and leave it at that.

Fitz maintained that a limited affair was better than none at all. He would see her even if they had to abandon any intimacy. That way he could be close to her and keep track of his son. He never told her that Will had stared him down at the creek earlier in the summer. Fitz was rightly convinced that Mattie would have ended the affair immediately if she had known that Will suspected anything. She was confident that Will was totally in the dark. If there was a hint that this was not the case, any hope of Fitz's for a continued relationship would come to an abrupt end.

The two of them sat in Fitz's Lincoln enjoying a warm breeze through the open windows. Tonight she had refused Fitz's invitation for more than conversation. Tonight was to be talk only. Carried high in the tall pines, the wind was a whisper. Then as the wind changed, the whisper turned into a moan. Mattie relaxed into the seat and laid her head back listening. A steady flow of water rushed past them in the creek.

"I don't see why we can't keep doing what we've been doing," Fitz made the same plea he had been making all summer.

"We have been over and over this. My mind is made up. My husband does not deserve being treated this way and I have to do what's best for my family," she explained again.

"You can't tell me that you don't love me. I know you do. You know how much I love you Mattie. I always have," Fitz said as he reached for another cigarette.

"You want one," he extended the pack to Mattie, who accepted. She exhaled smoke into the night.

"What about John," Fitz asked for the umpteenth time.

"What about him. I've told you that I will raise him in the family he knows. There is no need to deprive him of that," she answered.

"I want to help somehow. There must be a way for me to contribute without anyone else knowing about it. You could at least do that for me," he argued.

"It's not about you Fitz. Can't you understand? It's not about either of us. It's about three innocent people. It is up to us to protect all of them. You owe that much to Rebecca and me to Will. We both owe it to our son," Mattie countered.

"Oh to hell with Rebecca," he spat.

"Now you stop that. She loves you, the poor soul. I will not let you hurt her. She confided to me the belief that you are having an affair. She thinks its Tippy." In the distance a hoot owl "hoo-hooed" in the night, and it was time to go. Mattie allowed a kiss before departing for home. Will would be home from Hank's Place pretty soon and she had to get going. Going to Hank's on a Saturday night was ritual for Will, but not for Mattie. Sometimes these opportunities were used for their rendezvous.

After Mattie drove off, Fitz remained in his car smoking. He turned the radio on low and tuned it to a blues station from the Twin Cities. Periodically, he sipped from a flask. He wasn't going to give up that easy, but it would be weeks before she would see him again. The time between their brief encounters passed with excruciating slowness. The thought of going home to Rebecca made his stomach turn. Leaving Dismal Creek, Fitz drove to a friend's house for a little comfort. She was one of the women who never turned him away from a midnight visit.

Fitz settled in at the District Attorney's Office after his defeat at the polls, which was fine with him. The constant infighting in Madison over the most mundane things had left him bored and indifferent. It was in his capacity as an Assistant District Attorney that he learned about Will and Sonny's fight at Hank's. It would fall to him to determine whether any charges were in order. However, Fitz was not about to press this issue until he knew what had been said. When he called Mattie, she suggested a meeting at their usual spot.

On the evening of August 21, 1950, Fitz drove to the spot by the creek. A late afternoon rain had left the evening steamy. With no breeze, sitting in the car was not an option. It was just too hot. Fitz never went anywhere in the woods without his small caliber revolver which he now stuffed into his back pocket as he exited his vehicle. He took off his suit jacket, rolled up his sleeves, and loosened his tie, leaving his hat on the dashboard.

Leaning against the trunk of the Lincoln, Fitz smoked his cigarette in near total darkness. Low lying clouds blocked whatever star light was trying to get through. He waited for thirty minutes before he began to worry that Mattie wouldn't show up. After another half an hour crawled by he began to give up hope. Then he heard the sound of Mattie's coupe growing louder as it approached. Her way was illuminated only by parking lights and her progress was slow through the trees. When Fitz opened the door, Mattie held him for a long time.

"I'm scared. Sonny Howland has seen us together," she said to his chest where her cheek rested. Feeling her tremble against him, she felt delicate and fragile. Stroking her hair softly he whispered that everything would be alright. After long warm moments, they separated and Mattie accepted a cigarette. After a few drags of the cigarette she revealed her worry.

"He asked me if I'd been having sex with you here at the creek. Only he used vulgar language. I won't repeat that word."

"What did you say?"

"I called him a pig. Then the fight started."

Mattie went on to describe the fight and the aftermath at the house. When she refused to tell Will what Sonny had said, her husband became extremely angry. It was the only time Will ever raised his voice to her in all of their years together. Mattie refused to budge and left him with no choice but to accept her statement. Everyone knew her aversion to profanity and vulgarity. So when she insisted it was something a vile pig like Howland would say to a lady, Will relented.

"I wonder how much Howland knows," Fitz asked.

"It's impossible to say, but he must have seen us here together or he would not have said it. I just don't know what to do."

"He could make a lot of trouble for us. Maybe I need to talk to him, find out," Fitz suggested. They debated the issue for a while without coming to any conclusions.

"I better go. Are they going to arrest Will for the fight," she asked.

"Not if I have anything to say about it. I sure don't want anyone poking around in this mess. I'll recommend no charges in return for payment of the damages," he concluded. "But the final decision is up to the D.A."

"Good. Well, I'll see you. Thanks for meeting me," she gave him a goodbye kiss and turned to go.

Both Mattie and Fitz were blinded by the flashlight in their eyes. Raising their arms in defense, they squinted into the beam, frozen.

"Heh, heh, heh. Not very goddamn ladylike tonight, are we Mrs. Graves. And you Mr. District Attorney. You look like you're about to piss your pants."

For a long moment, they stood as if turned to stone. Finally, Fitz demanded that he shut the "damn light off."

"Go fuck yourself lawyer. You don't give the orders here. I do."

"What do you want," Fitz asked. They both knew it was Howland.

"What do I want? Let me see. To see you crawl and beg would be nice for starters. Maybe I want a big slice of all of that big shot money you got. Maybe I want a taste of what you been gettin' in the back seat of your car. Or maybe just seeing the two of you bleed. How 'bout that lawyer man," Howland said, mean and drunk.

"Over my dead body you son of a bitch," and with that Fitz pulled out his revolver and fired three rounds at the light which was dropped to the ground. Howland grunted and fell back against the car before rushing Fitz, knocking Mattie out of the way as he ran by her. Sonny slammed into Fitz and they landed in a tangle of arms on the ground. The flashlight illuminated the rolling and cursing men. Fitz was no match for the powerful experienced Howland and in no time he was on top of Fitz with his hands around his throat. Fitz felt Howland begin to squeeze the life out of him, seeing black spots and losing his breath. Losing consciousness, he saw the hatred on the man's face. Losing the battle for his own breath, Fitz heard a loud POP, then another.

A bewildered look crossed Howland's face as he collapsed onto Fitz. Scrambling and coughing, Fitz managed to push Howland away. When he finally regained his air, Fitz turned his attention to Mattie. She stood mute with the gun hanging in her hand by her side.

He went to her and gently removed the gun from her hand and returned it to his pocket. He made sure she was okay and then helped her into the front seat of her car. Checking to see that Howland was dead, he left him in a pile. Doing a quick search of the area he grabbed the flashlight and turned it off.

"Listen Mattie. Mattie, look at me," he bent towards her in the open doorway of her car. Mattie sat numb behind the wheel. Fitz lifted her chin towards him so he could look at her eyes.

"Mattie. Come on Mattie. You have got to snap out of this. It's over. He's dead. He would have killed us both."

Mattie emerged from her shock and began to sob. Fitz knelt down by her and took her into his arms, holding her long enough for the emotion to pass. It was quickly agreed that neither of them had done anything wrong. This was a clear case of self defense and they certainly felt justified under the circumstances.

But that conclusion did not begin to address the problem. They hatched a cover up, but agreed to come forward if it looked as though someone else was to get the blame. When the blame settled on Will, Mattie wanted to come forward immediately, but Fitz convinced her to wait. Although they did not see each other again until the day of Will's trial, they kept in phone contact. Fitz was prepared to fall on his sword and he told Mattie that if the trial went badly for Will, he would confess. Determined to protect Mattie and his son, Fitz promised that he would make no reference to Mattie.

Mattie insisted on the whole truth and refused to let him take the rap. Nothing could sway Fitz, however. For maybe the first time in his life he wore his manhood on his sleeve. In the face of his determination and his persuasive argument that she needed to take care of their son, she relented.

His cover story would be that he fell asleep reading poetry by the creek and woke up with Howland attempting to rob him. The claim would be self defense and he would take his chances that a jury would agree. The facts and the cover story were not true, but the motivation for shooting Howland was certainly real. Fitz and Mattie had feared for their lives in the menacing presence of Sonny Howland. There was no need to ruin the lives of Mattie and his son. Fortunately the need for the lie died with the dismissal of the charges against Will.

Following on the heels of the dismissal came the final goodbye. When she said it this time, Fitz honored the request and left her alone. His life's love and the only son he would ever have were lost to him forever. From then until he blew his brains out, Fitz stayed close to the scotch bottle.

"If you are wondering how I know all this in such detail, please be assured that Fitz discussed this night with me many times, Mr. Delaney," Tippy stated at the end of the story.

"One more thing that has been bothering me. Why would the widow give you Mr. Fitzgerald's picture, feeling the way she did?"

Tippy thought it was spite, speculating that Rebecca saw it as a slap in Tippy's face because she had believed Tippy was the scarlet woman.

Jack was exhausted and Tippy Gamble was finally drunk. With not much else to say he thanked her and left. Once he got into the truck he said "Jesus H. Christ" out loud. As he unlimbered Old Blue, Jack realized that the Howland case was finally solved. Fitz had plugged him and then Mattie had finished him off. Mattie Graves had shot the bastard and lived with it for the rest of her life never telling a soul. She had kept the secret to herself, raised her son, and buried her husband. During the process, she had maintained her friendship with the widow without so much as uttering a word about the affair or shooting. What a woman, Jack thought.

As he drove East on I-94 towards home he thought about the widow's tribute to Mattie at the funeral. "Man alive," Jack said to the windshield. After all these years Will Graves was finally cleared of Sonny Howland's murder. It gave Jack a great deal of satisfaction to know this fact. However, he could never reveal a word of it. He knew in his heart that Will Graves would not want the world to know that his beloved wife had killed a man while protecting her lover. Rather, Jack knew that Will would prefer to shoulder the blame.

He couldn't wait to tell Anna and reached for his cell phone. "Dammit," he said as he threw it back into the glove compartment with its dead battery. Jack had forgotten to turn it off. Oh well, he thought. He'd be home soon and the story would just have to wait. In his pocket Jack carried a copy of Fitz's last letter to Mattie. Fitz had given it to Tippy along with the Robinson poetry book.

# CHAPTER FORTY TWO

It puzzled Jack that the house was dark, but the note on the table provided the answer. On the way to the hospital, Jack asked Old Blue to give him all she had. There was no taking it easy on this trip. Foot to the floor, he roared along at the truck's top speed of 85 miles per hour.

He left the truck outside the emergency room door with its engine running and door open as he raced to the baby floor. The ward nurse saw him coming and led him to Anna's room. His wife was in the middle of a terrific labor pain. Her intensity and the task did not prevent her from seeing Jack enter the room. With the pain over, she reached for his hand which she placed in a human vice grip.

"Thank God you are here!" The relief on her face was palpable. He kissed her sweaty forehead and stroked her matted wet hair. Jack found his wife to be more beautiful than he had ever seen her.

Anna filled Jack in on all the baby details, reassuring him that everything was alright. Both Dr. Powers and the nurse brought him up to speed on the delivery, which was impending. When they were alone and before the next round of pain, Anna turned to Jack's St. Paul trip. "What kept you so long," she asked.

Jack was almost at a loss as to where to begin. First, he told her about Tippy and her connection to the widow. Then he walked her through an abbreviated version of the story as it was told to him. Then concluded, "Mattie had an affair with Thomas Fitzgerald. He's your grandfather."

"She was sure about this," Anna asked.

"Yeah, I'd say she was positive. Then there's this," Jack handed Anna a copy of the last letter written by Fitz which she read aloud.

"To my beloved,

Your last statements to me on the finality of your good-bye have left me bereft. In all the world you are the only woman I have ever loved. You are all that I ever wanted and I know that you loved me.

That I will never again see the moonlight reflected off your skin or feel your warmth beneath me is distressing beyond all measure. My poet's heart has been torn asunder and shall forever beat a cadence of sadness and longing.

Nevertheless I shall honor your wishes. As promised on that miserable day of goodbyes, this is the last you will ever hear from me.

Please take care of our son. He is such a wonderful little boy. When he is old enough please give him the Whitman book that accompanies this letter. At least he will have something from me.

You are the love of my life Mattie and it shall always remain so.

Eternally yours - Fitz."

Anna put down the letter and cried. When she had regained a little composure she said, "No wonder that picture of Thomas Fitzgerald looked familiar to me. He is my real grandfather." Shaking her head in near disbelief Anna added, "I know the Whitman book. It's on my dad's desk at home. There's an inscription of some sort inside the cover and it's signed 'your parents, with love'."

After a few more rounds of pain that seemed closer and more intense each time, Jack told Anna about the night at Dismal Creek. "So Grams shot Sonny Howland," she said with a certain amount of awe. "My grandmother. A Frost book in one hand and a gun in the other," she said in obvious incredulity. The image touched a funny bone and tripped the tension wire in each of them, releasing waves of laughter. Then it was time to go to the delivery room. As Anna was seized by the last paroxysm of labor pain, the medical team assembled for the birth.

"Okay honey. The baby's on its way. Push," the doctor instructed. "Come on. Push," she prodded again.

"Uhhhhhhhhhh!" Anna pushed and grunted.

"Here comes the crown. Push. One more big push and... there you go...here she comes...okay, now for the shoulders. Take a breath," the doctor coaxed. Anna panted and then took a gulp of air and pushed again.

"Uhhhhhhhhhh!!"

"Here she is. She's through. Oh, my she's beautiful," the doctor gushed.

Anna laid back exhausted with tears flowing down her cheeks and laughing at the same time. Jack kissed her. He had to steady himself. The experience of watching his daughter being born was overwhelming. The doctor held up Mattie Anne for Anna to see.

"Oh my, oh my, oh...," at that moment, as Anna reached for her baby, she collapsed and the monitors began to wail that something had gone terribly wrong.

Mattie Anne was whisked away by a nurse and Jack was pushed out of the way by the doctor. In a flurry of activity the assembled medical team turned its collective attention to the mother who was in obvious cardiac arrest. But all of their combined efforts were to no avail.

The autopsy revealed that Anna had died instantly from an amniotic fluid embolism. Extremely rare, unpreventable, unpredictable, and deadly, an amniotic fluid embolism occurs when the amniotic fluid or fetal material enters the mother's blood stream. There was nothing anyone could have done. Death was instantaneous.

Jack's anguish ruled his world. His bereavement snuffed out all of the joy from his being. Throughout the wake and funeral he was present only in the physical sense of the word. The best he could do was to accept the condolences of those around him. Nothing brought him comfort, however. That part of the heart that accepts the thoughts, prayers, and kindness of others was as dead as his beloved wife. Numb, slain by the loss, his heart shattered, Jack Delaney entered the darkness of a joyless life.

# EPILOGUE

Frost covered the world below the mound as a hint of red colored the eastern sky. Cool air carried on the late autumn breeze ruffled Harry and Jack's hair. In the five years since Anna's death, change had come to Stoney Lonesome Road.

Harry laid his big head over Jack's shoulder and gave him a head hug. He licked Jack's ear and in return received hugs and scratches until he lay down and put his head in Jack's lap. Without his dog Jack was pretty sure he would not have made it following Anna's death. It had felt as though his entire insides had been ripped out and had been replaced with a painful hollowness that refused to go away.

When he was able to muster enough strength, Jack spent months in Washburn. Alternating between parenthood and despair, he went to the little cabin on Lake Superior where he and Anna had stayed. Man and dog would sit the rock and feel the spray as the owner played "Amazing Grace" to the morning. Wherever Jack went, Harry went too. Except for breakfast at the Time Out café, Jack kept to himself on these trips up north. While he was in Washburn, Jack drank deeply from the Artesian well in the park.

When he was away Cindy cared for Mattie Anne. Without expectation or reward, Cindy had closed the bar and stepped in to mother Mattie Anne. Jack had accepted her help and through the

fog of his pain was grateful. Without Cindy to hold on to the pieces of his broken life, Jack was sure he would have come completely
unglued. She was there for him like always. Her comforting presence gave Jack a soft place to lay his grief. When he needed to parent, she showed him how. When it was necessary to get away, she
packed his clothes. When he cried, she held him.

Fortunately for Jack and Mattie Anne, Cindy was a natural
mother. She read her stories and took Mattie Anne on adventures
all over the farm. The little girl called her mom. Cindy loved
Mattie Anne unconditionally as if she were her child.

The curly haired little girl's green eyes brightened while listening to stories. Her favorite story was about a mother and a daughter named Anna who lived on a farm far away. She named her
favorite doll Anna and refused to go anywhere without her.

As Jack's pain ebbed, he spent increasing amounts of time with
Mattie Anne. It wasn't long before Mattie Anne went with him
wherever he went. She would scrunch up against him on the seat
while Harry sat next to her with his head out the window.

Jack took a deep breath and then turned his face toward the
morning sun. Its first rays caused the frost covered trees to spar-
kle. From his view point it looked like a shimmering crystal sea.
Even with such beauty before him, the universe would never be
the same.

To help fill the void of Anna's loss, Jack Delaney did what he
had always done to fill the loneliness. He got back in the squad
car and went to work.

As the sun rose higher, it shone against the big red barn which
had been rebuilt to its original glory. Jack used old pictures and
his memory to recreate Will Grave's barn. Jack thought rebuilding
the barn was the least he could do for Will. The only help he had
had in the rebuilding was Herb. One day as Jack was laying the
foundation to the barn, Herb showed up to help. Then he showed
up the next day and the next and the next. Once the barn was

finished, Herb started in on the other buildings. Then he turned his attention to the fences and the fields.

From the mound Jack saw customers pulling into the parking lot of what used to be Hank's Place. Now a neon lit convenience store occupied the corner. And Jack had to admit it was handy to have the store in the neighborhood.

Stoney Lonesome Road had been widened, straightened, and striped from one end to the other. Even his front yard had suffered when the road was widened. The county had also straightened out the sharp S curve and the road now ran through what used to be Doyle's trailer. There was nothing left of the man or his place.

Jack was glad that he had had the chance to tell Anna the truth about her real grandfather and the murder of Sonny Howland. When Mattie Anne was ready, Jack would tell her the story as well. In the meantime, he had written a full report and put it in his private file along with the photo of Thomas Fitzgerald.

It's funny how things work out, Jack thought. Not too long after Anna's death, Adde had called him about the untimely demise of Tippy Gamble. Apparently Tippy had one too many spiked drinks and failed to negotiate the stairway, falling to the floor beneath her photo. But with her customary style, Tippy made a bequest to the University, stipulating that the money was for a Chair in honor of Thomas Fitzgerald.

With the sun up and work to do, Jack and Harry made their way back to the cemetery where the trail ended. He stopped and wiped the frost off Anna's headstone so he could clearly see the inscription. She had been buried next to her grandparents with a simple stone. The inscription read "Nothing Gold Can Stay."

Author Rick Pendergast was born on a small Wisconsin dairy farm to parents who survived the Great Depression. They taught him the value of hard work and the dangers of judging people based on first impressions. These lessons of perseverance and compassion served Pendergast well during his careers in the air force, law enforcement, and the law.

After being honorably discharged from the air force, Pendergast earned a degree in political science with a minor in English.

Pendergast was a policeman on the Eau Claire Police Department before leaving to attend law school. After graduation, he returned home to practice law.

Pendergast lives with his wife, Ellen, in a country house they built on the corner of the family farm. They have seven children, fourteen grandchildren, and two great-grandchildren between them.

Made in the USA
Lexington, KY
18 June 2018